"My price is a date

Marissa gazed up at K̶̶̶̶̶ her head. "I can't. What kind of matchmaker would swoop in and take the prize catch for herself? No client would ever trust me again."

Upping his game, Kyle raised a finger to her face and sketched a soft stroke down the length of her throat.

Her eyelids fluttered, her lips parting of their own accord.

"What are we doing?" she whispered helplessly, clutching his shoulders as if she were hanging on for dear life.

"Being impulsive." He licked his way into the curve of her shoulder and she shivered. "Isn't it the best?"

"I'm not impulsive," she said, even as she arched her neck to give him more room to work.

He ran his tongue along that same spot over and over until she trembled again.

"You are now."

Blaze

Dear Reader,

As if being married to a former sports editor didn't fill my life with enough sports talk, I'm also raising three highly competitive sons. Team sports fill my days and reviewing game film often occupies our time between game days. It's a fun family pastime and has given me lots of insight into all kinds of sports.

I've written baseball players for Blaze in *Double Play* and *Sliding into Home*. But my new series takes me to the world of hockey—which some readers may recall I touched on back in 2004 in *Date with a Diva*.

Welcome to Double Overtime, where hockey reigns supreme and hot athletes abound. What makes the stories all the more fun is the connection to the Murphy family, which I introduced in last fall's linked Wrong Bed books *Making a Splash* and *Riding the Storm.* The Murphys are a family of five brothers and their foster brother, Axel, who gets a story next month in *Her Man Advantage.*

I sure hope you'll enjoy these sports heroes as much as I've enjoyed writing them. Most of all, thank you for picking up one of my books and giving me the chance to share a story with you!

Happy reading,

Joanne Rock

Joanne Rock

ONE MAN RUSH

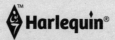

TORONTO NEW YORK LONDON
AMSTERDAM PARIS SYDNEY HAMBURG
STOCKHOLM ATHENS TOKYO MILAN MADRID
PRAGUE WARSAW BUDAPEST AUCKLAND

Recycling programs
for this product may
not exist in your area.

ISBN-13: 978-0-373-79682-3

ONE MAN RUSH

www.Harlequin.com

Printed in U.S.A.

ABOUT THE AUTHOR

The mother of three sports-minded sons, Joanne Rock has found her primary occupation to be carting kids to practices and cheering on their athletic prowess at any number of sporting events. In the windows of time between football games, she loves to write and cheer on happily-ever-afters. A three-time RITA® Award nominee, Joanne is the author of more than fifty books for a variety of Harlequin series. She has been an *RT Book Reviews* Career Achievement Award nominee and multiple Reviewers' Choice finalist including a nomination for *Making a Splash* (Blaze #636) as Best Blaze of 2011. Her work has been reprinted in twenty-six countries and translated into nineteen languages. Over two million copies of her books are in print. For more information on Joanne's books, visit www.joannerock.com.

Books by Joanne Rock

HARLEQUIN BLAZE
171—SILK CONFESSIONS
182—HIS WICKED WAYS
240—UP ALL NIGHT
256—HIDDEN OBSESSION
305—DON'T LOOK BACK
311—JUST ONE LOOK
363—A BLAZING
      LITTLE CHRISTMAS
  "His for the Holidays"
381—GETTING LUCKY
395—UP CLOSE AND PERSONAL
450—SHE THINKS HER EX IS SEXY...
457—ALWAYS READY
486—SLIDING INTO HOME
519—MANHUNTING
  "The Takedown"
534—THE CAPTIVE
560—DOUBLE PLAY
582—UNDER WRAPS
604—HIGHLY CHARGED!
636—MAKING A SPLASH
643—RIDING THE STORM

HARLEQUIN HISTORICAL
749—THE BETROTHAL
  "Highland Handfast"
758—MY LADY'S FAVOR
769—THE LAIRD'S LADY
812—THE KNIGHT'S COURTSHIP
890—A KNIGHT MOST WICKED
942—THE KNIGHT'S RETURN

For my sons, Taylor, Camden and Maxim.
Thank you for the love, the laughs,
and for occasionally cleaning your rooms.
I could not be more proud of you boys!

1

MARISSA COLLINS WAS IN the market for a man. A tall, dark and gorgeous man. In fact, she'd set her sights on Philadelphia's most wanted eligible bachelor.

Snagging that kind of prize target might intimidate most women. But since her work as a personal matchmaker had Marissa chasing single guys on a daily basis, tonight's manhunt was all in a day's work.

Handing her keys to the valet in front of the Normandy Farm Hotel in the Philadelphia suburbs, Marissa stepped out of the cramped hybrid car and stretched her legs at the scene of her evening's mission. A tension headache that had started this morning after another call from a high-priority client twisted into a throbbing knot behind her eye. Hockey superstar Kyle Murphy was on her top client's personal Most Wanted list, and Marissa had no choice but to deliver if she was going to keep her customer happy. Ever since her mother had been injured, Marissa no longer worked as a matchmaker just for the love of it. Being her mom's primary caretaker necessitated an income.

"Enjoy your evening, ma'am." The college kid in a

bow tie and windbreaker grinned at her as she gathered her purse and an evening wrap to ward off the chill of a March evening.

She handled the silk chiffon carefully, the white showstopper a long-ago gift from her mother. Brandy Collins, her pop singer mom, had bought it while on tour in Italy back when she commanded standing-room-only audiences—before the traumatic brain injury that left her frequently confused and fighting to retain basic motor skills. There were experimental medicines available, but without FDA approval, Marissa needed funds to afford the care. She'd give anything to see the light of real recognition in her mom's eyes again.

"Can you tell me which way to the Philadelphia Phantoms event?" she asked the valet as he slid behind the wheel of her vehicle.

She dug into her purse for a pair of rhinestone earrings and clipped them into place.

"The hockey team is in the main conference atrium." The valet pointed as he checked for traffic near the unloading area. "There are signs when you walk in."

"Thanks." She hurried toward the main entrance between pillars wrapped in white lights, then took one last peek at the newspaper article in her evening bag.

Phantoms' Playmaker Wins Shootout, the headline announced in a piece that ran in the sports section yesterday. But the text wasn't as important as the photo of the team's playmaker himself—power forward Kyle Murphy.

"You look like trouble to me," she muttered, taking note of the hockey star's square jaw and high cheekbones. Forest-green eyes glimmered with good humor while a slightly crooked nose prevented him from being Bachelor of the Month gorgeous. Every other trait belonging to Kyle Murphy was handsome as sin and surely as much trouble.

An opinion Marissa had no problem sharing with her client, local celebutante Stacy Goodwell. But Stacy, the daughter of the obscenely wealthy owner of the Phantoms' arena, hadn't cared the athlete had a reputation for arrogance. According to Stacy, the player's hotness factor was off the charts. Her father had been willing to pay well above Marissa's usual commission to arrange this particular date.

Folding the article back down into the bottom of her bag, Marissa took out one last accessory before she went to work. She slid a plain gold band on her left hand and snapped the purse shut. Some women took off real wedding rings before a night on the town. Marissa suspected she was one of the few who slipped on a fake one. But it helped speed along conversations with single, eligible men when they knew she wasn't in the market for a date. Besides, any guy who didn't respect a wedding ring wasn't the kind of man she'd want for her clients.

"Welcome, miss." A gray-haired hotel employee in a dark suit opened the door for her.

She gave him a nod as she stepped into the facility and strode toward the conference center, determined to sign on Kyle and hoping that he and Stacy were truly a good match. She'd gotten into this job because she worked well behind the scenes, orchestrating other people's lives far more effectively than her own. She didn't want to lose that personal touch now just because financial need had entered the picture. But her mother needed those meds. She deserved a chance to recover her past and her memories. Surely the hockey player could agree to just one date with Stacy. It wasn't as though she was peddling her services to him for a fee since she already had a paying client in hand. She just needed Kyle to agree to a date.

Eighties rock music played by a DJ filtered through open double doors as she reached the atrium where the event was being held, the insistent guitar distinguishable even though the crowd noise swelled.

Rich red walls warmed the long corridor filled with people taking a break from the dance floor or escaping the music to talk. The party was in full swing, a fundraiser for a local children's hospital, with the main attraction being the opportunity to meet Phantoms players.

"Excuse me," Marissa all but shouted as the throng around the doors seemed oblivious.

The sea of bodies moved slightly, giving her room to bypass the social yakkers. A huge chandelier hung over the dance floor in a large hall designed to look more like a barn than a run-of-the-mill meeting space. For that matter, it *had* been a barn at one time. The high ceiling and rough wood beams of the original space remained.

But where was Kyle Murphy? Scanning the scene, she plotted how to approach a sought-after athlete. To be wealthy, powerful, talented and gorgeous had to be too many blessings for any one person to handle, a condition she'd witnessed in her time navigating her mother's former world—the insane culture of pop music. While

Marissa had never fit into the craziness and excess, she'd cobbled together a network of friends in her travels. Those same friends were her clients today thanks to a couple of great matches she'd made among her nearest and dearest back in the days before she charged for her skills.

"May I get you anything, hon?" a frizzy-haired blonde waitress asked as she tucked an empty serving tray under one arm.

"No, thank you." Waiting for a drink at the bar would be a better way to scope out the bash.

Marissa headed toward the line at a freestanding bar in the corner of the room. With some more perspective on the party, she could see a few Phantoms players seated at signing tables against a back wall. No doubt that's where they'd stationed Kyle Murphy.

Could she outlast the line and corner him after he'd dispensed with the fan meet-and-greet? When he didn't have twenty people around?

Racking her brain for a plan to get him alone without crossing into stalker territory, Marissa was suddenly next up at the bar.

Still with no strategy in sight.

"Can I have a Diet Coke?" she asked the bartender as the women who'd been in front of her finally giggled their way back to the dance floor. The high-octave girly laughter raked along Marissa's already tense nerves, cranking up the ache behind her left eyeball. "Actually, could you add a Macallan over ice to that order?"

She'd be stuck here for a couple of hours if she wanted to wait out the crowds. A little whiskey might take some of the meanness out of the headache, at least.

"I don't know," the bartender shot back with a deep bass, drawing her attention from the mob around the hockey players. "Can I see some ID?"

Frowning, Marissa knew she didn't look remotely close to the minimum drinking age. If anything, she dressed like someone a couple of decades older than her twenty-seven years in an effort to keep herself out of the fray when it came to discussing dates. Still, she reached for her purse to retrieve her license, her gaze moving toward the guy behind the bar who was dressed incongruously in a crisp white tuxedo shirt and a base-ball cap.

Forest-green eyes glittered back at her in the icy flu-orescent glow from a lamp on the bar. A crooked nose hovered above full, sculpted lips. Even with a Phantoms cap pulled low over his forehead, the shape of the bar-tender's face remained familiar, perhaps because she'd studied it in a newspaper clipping so recently.

The Phantoms' playmaker stood right in front of her.

She'd wanted a one-on-one with power forward Kyle Murphy. Unfortunately, the sudden appearance of so much potent sex appeal robbed her of speech, thought and good sense.

Silence stretched while her heartbeat thundered.

As professional first impressions went, she couldn't imagine making a worse one.

No words were necessary when sexual attraction spoke a language all its own.

Kyle Murphy enjoyed the moment as he assessed the reed-thin female on the other side of the bar who'd been struck speechless ever since he'd asked for her ID.

The old-fashioned tortoiseshell cat's-eye frames that perched on her nose were vintage 1960s. In fact, she looked as though she could have stepped off the set of *Mad Men* with her vintage dress and perfectly applied lipstick. Her dark hair was yanked back in an unforgiving twist rarely worn by young women.

Her style seemed purposely quirky. But if she intended to hide behind the glasses and the severe hairstyle, she'd failed miserably. Dressing twenty years older than she was didn't disguise her subtle curves. If anything, the clothes accentuated her hips and her narrow waist. Sometimes the more a woman covered up, the more a guy noticed. Especially when the rest of the women in the room were dressed in spaghetti straps and short skirts. Besides, this female had pretty features. High, arched brows topped off eyes so blue they were practically violet. A slightly upturned nose gave her a patrician look. Creamy, pale skin contrasted sharply with inky dark hair.

Sexy. Unusual. And the first woman who hadn't ordered an appletini or a cosmo in the half hour he'd manned the bar.

She was the kind of woman that appealed to him— the kind who didn't look as if she was trying too hard. But he reminded himself that he was done with casual hookups. First of all because it was deep into the hockey season and he needed to be focused on his game. He hadn't been with anyone since last autumn, when he'd convinced one of the nurses on an opponent's medical staff to come home with him. Turned out she'd only been in the market to see how many pro athlete conquests she could make and she was gone before dawn. So he planned to be more careful with dating when he got back around to it—after he took home the Stanley Cup this spring.

After a long deer-in-the-headlights look, the woman at the bar finally spoke.

"I'm sorry." She shook her head as if to clear it. "On second thought, I definitely don't need the alcohol. Diet Coke will be fine."

"I was only messing with you about the ID," he confided, taking his time with the ice cubes so he could keep her there longer. Figure out what it was that drew his attention like a magnet. "Anyone who rakes in enough dough to warrant a plate at this party deserves a drink."

He wasn't the kind to flirt, so he didn't understand why he found himself sliding closer than necessary to speak to her. Her whole bookworm vibe was an intriguing change from the women who threw themselves at him because of his job. But he had no business getting attached to anyone when he was on the road for most of the year and could be traded at any time. He'd been in Philly for less than a month after playing in Boston for most of the season. For all he knew, he could be on the roster in Edmonton this time next year. The Phantoms had wanted the scoring magic he offered in tandem with his foster brother, Axel Rankin. The two of them had been reunited on the ice at the start of the season when Kyle had started the year with Axel's former team, the Boston Bears. They'd each posted record-breaking stats with the club, but had been picked up by the Phantoms at the trade deadline when the Bears showed no signs of making a play-off run.

"Anyone talented enough to make an NHL roster deserves to enjoy a team soirée rather than work the bar."

"Shh." He put a finger over his lips, wanting her to keep a lid on his secret, and cracked open a soda from a nearby cooler. "Not many people have spotted me over here yet."

"You like downplaying your role?" Her eyebrows knitted, as if she found that hard to believe.

"I prefer to let my stickhandling do my talking." He cut a fresh lemon and tossed a slice in the glass, still stalling and determined to make the most of this little moment. "I'm not much on the dog-and-pony-show promo events, but this is different since it's for a group of the Phantoms' charities. Still, I'd rather offer up manpower behind the bar than sign hats or total strangers' breasts."

He couldn't imagine this woman digging under a T-shirt to offer up her wares at a public autographing event, and that made him all the more interested in earning the privilege to see them privately.

A ghost of a smile played along her lips so quickly he wasn't sure it had even been there. She leaned over the bar just enough to lower her voice.

"Aren't you a little young for the thrill of strange breasts to have worn off already?" She eyeballed him above the rim of those librarian glasses, and he felt latent naughty-teacher fantasies spring to life.

"In my experience, the best things in life don't come easy." He topped off the soda she'd ordered, unable to stall any longer with a scowling, red-faced guy in a tux in line behind her. "I'd rather invest the time necessary to do the undressing myself."

She eased back, nodding her approval. "Very commendable. You are a welcome surprise, Mr. Murphy."

"Kyle," he corrected her, feeling as though she'd just pasted a gold star to his forehead in front of the whole class. He couldn't recall the last time anyone had called his actions commendable. "Here you go, Ms.—"

He passed her drink to her.

"Marissa Collins. And thank you." She reached for the glass, her fingers grazing his for one electric moment before she drew back.

He had the urge to ditch the barkeeping duties and pull Marissa Collins into a dark corner.

"Marissa, I finish up here in an hour. Can I interest you in that glass of scotch at around ten?" He hardly ever drank during the season and never on a game night. But he had tomorrow off, and he'd take any excuse to spend a little longer with the unusual beauty who made him think about something besides hockey for the first time in a long time. Not to take her home. Just to talk.

Before she could answer, his gaze fell on her left hand as she reached into an evening bag for a few bills to pay for her soda. A shiny gold band winked at him from her ring finger.

He shouldn't be surprised. She'd struck him as more aloof than the women he usually met. But he'd assumed she was just self-assured.

"Never mind," he corrected himself, right about the same time she said, "Sounds great."

He guessed his expression must be a mirror of her frown. Damn it. Didn't she see anything wrong in having a drink with him when she was already taken?

Shutting down thoughts of Marissa Collins as fast as possible, he ignored the money she slid across the bar, turning instead to the sweaty and cranky-looking customer who'd been fidgeting impatiently behind her.

"May I help you, sir?" he asked, realizing the guy didn't recognize him as a player and therefore didn't appreciate having to wait so long for a drink.

Right now, Kyle was just another working stiff whose flirtation with a pretty girl hadn't amounted to anything. He shouldn't feel any different from when he left the hat signings and the female fans who hoped for hookups he'd rarely indulged.

But regret burned now in a way it never had before. With an effort, he kept his eyes off Marissa as she disappeared into the crowd. The last thing he wanted to see was her with some guy who had the right to call her his.

2

No matter that Marissa had always worked hard to take herself out of the equation when it came to arranging dates, she had been sucked in by Kyle Murphy with just one look.

What had happened back there?

Chugging her cola as if it were some magic elixir that could bring her back to sanity, she felt as though she was shaking from the aftershocks of a cataclysmic event. No wait, that was her phone vibrating away in her purse. She ducked into a corner of the room to check her messages, telling herself all the while to forget her strange reaction to the hockey star. She was a healthy, red-blooded female with little to no love life to speak of. Was it any wonder she occasionally got tripped up by the sight of an appealing man?

Although tripped up wasn't exactly accurate. More like knocked stupid by a two by four to the head.

Cursing herself and hormones that only got in the way of her job, she yanked her phone free from her purse and saw a terse text:

Where R U?

Did no one bother with hello anymore, let alone identifying themselves? She squinted in the dark to read the numbers on the display. A local call.

The buzzing sounded again, along with a new message.

Have U found him?

It had to be Stacy, the client who wanted desperately to meet Kyle. Frustration heated through her while the dance floor erupted with cheers at the opening strains of "Cotton Eyed Joe."

Plunking out a response on tiny keys, she reminded Stacy that she would be in touch with news next week. In the meantime, another text came through.

Am by autograph tables. I don't C him!!

Marissa stopped in the middle of typing to peer around the room. And, crap, there was Stacy's asymmetrical platinum-blond bob, a standout in any crowd. The bright, shiny hair topped off a silver metallic dress and neon-blue vinyl heels.

Stacy was bending low over a table to have a giveaway hat signed by a player Marissa didn't recognize. Her posture brought to mind Marissa's conversation with Kyle. His comment about being offered strangers' breasts. Damn it, why couldn't Stacy have stayed home and waited for her introduction so Marissa could have coached her on making a positive impression? She hated the little voice in her head reminding her Kyle had flirted with *her,* so she must have made a good impression. The last thing she needed were personal feelings getting mixed up in a must-do business deal.

Pocketing the phone, Marissa marched toward the client who was determined to give her ulcers.

"Stacy." She reached the other woman's side and tugged her away from a hulking Czech player whose face was stitched up like a football. "Will you excuse us?"

"Marissa!" Stacy hugged her, an oversize cocktail ring catching Marissa's hair while the woman's silver sequins snagged on the silk shawl Marissa wore. "Have you found him? Does he want to meet me?"

Stacy looked flustered. Embarrassed at having been caught chatting up another player when she was trying to arrange a date with Kyle Murphy? Marissa couldn't tell. But when Stacy yanked back, she dragged half the evening wrap with her while Marissa tried to pluck the delicate fabric free without tearing it.

"Hang on," she warned, knowing Stacy's uncanny ability to wreak havoc wherever she went. Oddly, her tendency toward clumsiness was part of her charm since it softened a personality that seemed—at first glance—a touch abrasive.

Twenty-four-year-old Stacy Goodwell was noisy, effusive, careless and utterly good-hearted. A writer for the Living section of the local paper, she spoke first and thought later, which was half the reason she needed a matchmaker. The other reason was that, while she was both rich and drop-dead gorgeous, she could be naive when it came to men. She tended to fall in love indiscriminately with guys who didn't have her best interests at heart.

She was a beautiful, lovable mess, and Marissa felt for her because her father was a pompous, overbearing gazillionaire who tried his best to run Stacy's life. He cared more about seeing her paired off with someone well-connected than someone who loved her. Sweet-natured Stacy hadn't quite figured out how to tell her father to stay out of her life, but for now she and her father agreed Kyle Murphy would be a great choice.

Mr. Goodwell was keen on Kyle because he was a wealthy, famous athlete and Goodwell liked to hobnob with that sort of person. Stacy had agreed, Marissa supposed, because Kyle was gorgeous and had a reputation for being charming—something Marissa had seen firsthand.

"Look at me!" Stacy laughed and her throaty humor drew stares from all the men within a ten-yard radius. "I'm here for five minutes and I'm already wrecking things."

Marissa freed herself with only a little damage done to the wrap. Frazzled and still reeling from her encounter with Kyle, she tucked her arm around Stacy's waist and drew her toward the ladies' room.

"You're fine. But can we talk somewhere?" She peered around the room and her eyes connected with Kyle's as if drawn by magnetic force.

Holy heat wave. The momentary connection was so sultry it curled her hair.

She didn't know who whipped their head away faster—her or him. Apparently, he was as determined as her to write off their little moment of sexual chemistry insanity. She needed to reroute his eyes toward Stacy, pronto.

"Of course," her client agreed, teetering carefully on her sky-high blue stiletto heels. "I finished my feature piece on the season's new hemlines early tonight, so my father encouraged me to be here in case you were ready to make an introduction—"

"No." Marissa shook her head to emphasize the point. Stopping at an empty table shoved against one wall, she pulled a chair over for Stacy. "I know you're anxious for this, but good relationships aren't something you race into. I need time to screen him—"

"That's okay." Stacy's blue eyes were as wide and earnest as a Japanese anime character. "He has a good reputation in the league, so the screening doesn't matter."

"It does." In fact, Marissa had spoken with Stacy's father about this point, since he was footing the bill for the matchmaking even though Stacy had wanted to go it alone. "I can gather information that will help make a date successful, okay?"

Assuming Marissa could get her head out of fantasy land and stop seeing Kyle through the fog of attraction that had struck her speechless earlier.

"Marissa." Stacy peered around and then leaned close to speak more softly. "I really need this date. My dad is putting on the pressure about settling down."

The idea bugged Marissa since Stacy didn't need to settle down at twenty-four. More likely, her father simply wanted to make the business connection with Kyle Murphy of Murphy family fame. The Murphys owned a global resort chain, a fact that might bring lucrative business toward Goodwell, who owned arenas worldwide.

"Which is why we should focus some of our search on men who are at a point in their lives where they're really interested in a commitment—"

"My dad thinks the world of Kyle Murphy," Stacy reminded her, those blue eyes tracking around the room as if she could find her dream date if she searched long enough. "Kyle has talked to my father about sponsoring a youth hockey camp for underprivileged kids and Dad thinks it's great. Plus, despite my protests, he's already hired a few other matchmakers to make sure I have a chance with Kyle."

Marissa reeled. Honestly, she was fortunate she hadn't worn heels or she might have toppled over at that bit of news. The revelation applied so much pressure on her, she felt lightheaded.

"You're kidding." Sure, she admired the idea of starting a youth hockey camp. But for Stacy's father to go after Kyle with such a heavy hand?

Stacy shrugged. "I wish I was, because I'd rather work with you, and I wanted dating to be one area of my life that I kept my father out of. But once my dad gets an idea in his head…" She shuddered. "It's next to impossible to talk him out of it. At least, I've never had much luck in that department."

Great. So the almighty Phil Goodwell called all the shots for his daughter's romantic future. However, by creating unhealthy competition and putting the focus on a specific end result rather than on the journey to true love, he wouldn't be doing her any favors. Did the man have any idea at all how matchmaking worked?

Marissa was in the business to help people find soul mates and to bring lasting happiness, not to arrange specific introductions dictated by heavy-handed coercion.

"I'm not going to second-guess your father's approach, but this is an unorthodox way to work." Read: completely ludicrous. "Remember that you want to find a relationship that will make you happy, and ultimately it's your decision."

Stacy's smile slipped for a moment and Marissa wondered if she'd gotten through to her. What daughter wouldn't balk at the idea of her father buying off her dates?

"But I think Kyle is great, too." Stacy pounded the table for emphasis, knocking over a glass of melting ice someone had left behind. "Sorry!"

Marissa edged her knees aside so the cold water could drip off the edge of the table unimpeded.

"Excuse me." A young man approached the table, his eyes lingering on Stacy's cleavage while a series of diamond studs winked above one eyebrow. "Would you like to dance?"

Stacy brightened, the spilled drink forgotten. "I'd love to." Then, sobering, she turned back to Marissa. "Is that okay?"

They were three years apart in age, but to Marissa it felt more like twenty-three. How had she become such a wise old sage before she'd turned thirty? Even before her mother's accident, she'd been a serious person. Now she divided her time between care-giving and negotiating dates for women who actually had lives.

But then, it was easier to orchestrate love from the sidelines than to navigate that rocky terrain for yourself. Sometimes Marissa wondered if that was half the reason she'd gotten into this business in the first place. Sure, she made other people happy. But standing in the wings also meant never risking a broken heart.

"Of course. But after that, I hope you'll consider going home." She lowered her voice and whispered in Stacy's ear. "Alone."

Rolling her eyes, Stacy trotted away with Diamond Brow, clinging to his arm so she didn't fall off her stiletto heels.

Marissa lifted her glasses and tucked them on top of her head so she could pinch the bridge of her nose. The tension had moved from her left eye to center between them. When she'd gotten into matchmaking, it had been about the fun of bringing two people together who really belonged with each other. Back then, she'd seen the job as a fun side interest to her main job of overseeing her mother's career. Brandy Collins, before her car accident, hadn't been all that different from Stacy Goodwell—charming and completely impractical. And she fired managers as easily as she agreed to random gigs without ever checking her schedule.

After Marissa finished college, it had seemed a natural fit to help her mother manage her career, especially after a financial advisor had absconded with a sizable portion of her mom's fortune. Someone needed to make sure no crackpots has access to her mother. But matchmaking had been one arena that was hers alone, and she'd really enjoyed it. Eventually, she'd started a private, personalized matchmaking service catering to an elite client base—wealthy singles who either didn't have enough time to meet new people or who had trouble meeting the *right* people. But Marissa had a knack for bringing couples together. Her theory was that seeing a good match required objectivity. But who could be objective when you were wildly attracted to someone?

Anyhow, she loved the job. She'd just never antici-
pated a day when it would become a high pressure, do-
or-die proposition. Like now. What would she do if one
of the competing matchmakers swooped in and wooed
away the Goodwell business? The depleted Collins' cof-
fers couldn't afford the hit.

"You really look like you could use that drink." The
male voice emanated from just above her right ear.

She didn't need to look to know who it was. Her
whole body hummed in recognition, reminding her of
the second biggest problem of the night.

Despite the fact that she needed to win over Kyle for
Stacy, Marissa wanted him for herself.

She opened her eyes to find the man of the hour
standing mere inches away, a tumbler in hand. He held
the amber liquid out to her, the ice cubes clinking.

Deep green eyes regarded her left hand for a moment
before they darted north to meet her gaze.

Left hand?

She looked at the place his stare had vacated and
spied her fake wedding band. Her thumb went auto-
matically to the thin gold, smoothing it absently.

"I'm not hitting on you," he assured her, seeming to
catch the gesture. "If anything, I wanted to apologize
for asking you to have a drink with me before. I didn't
realize you were, ah—married."

Marissa recalled the way he'd shuffled her aside
so abruptly. She'd been so caught off guard by her attraction earlier that she hadn't even fully processed
what had happened during that encounter. And while
it would be really convenient to hide behind that wed-

ding band, she felt strange overtly lying to him when his expression seemed so sincere.

"I'm not, actually." She reached to accept the drink.

He yanked it away.

"Hey, I'm trying to do the right thing by you, okay?" His brows plunged together at an ominous slant. "I don't touch married women."

His protest only charmed her more.

"That's admirable." She rose to her feet, hoping to clear the air with him so they could get down to business. "I wouldn't expect you to touch me either way, Mr. Murphy. Do you have a moment to speak somewhere privately? I only need a moment of your time."

The sharp angle to those eyebrows lifted. Arched. He seemed to consider stepping outside with her. Then his frown became more marked. He slammed her drink on the table she'd just vacated.

"Absolutely not. I'm flattered, but I take wedding vows seriously, and so should you." He folded his arms and made like an immovable wall, possibly to show her that she had a snowball's chance in hell of getting him to go anywhere with her.

Absurdly, her wayward gaze fell to the pronounced line of strong biceps and square shoulders, his body a gorgeous testament to the results of hard work. And she'd bet her open ogling would not help her cause. Where the heck was her usual reserve?

The last person she'd ever get involved with romantically was someone in the public eye. She'd taken a backseat to her mother's career forever. She knew better than to put herself in that same position with a man.

"That's fine." She spied a handful of guests headed

their way, giveaway hats and Sharpie markers in hand. "But I really would like to just speak with you. No touching. Do you think we could step into the hall for a minute?"

His eyes darted to the oncoming group. It was clear they hadn't identified him yet, but his size had drawn their attention and they craned their necks for a better view.

"This way." He tucked her under his arm, surprising her with his sudden proximity. "We can sit out on the terrace."

One hand gripping her shoulder, he steered her through the crowd, using his body to clear a path. The warmth of his fingers drifted through the silk of her evening wrap, soaking into her skin and making her feel...too many things to count. Secure. Aroused. Vibrantly alive.

Dragging in a deep breath as her feet stepped faster to keep up, Marissa inhaled the scent of him—she detected a slight hint of spicy aftershave, the starch in his tuxedo shirt and the undiluted masculine musk of the skin beneath.

The ballroom trappings disappeared, the light brightening and then darkening again as he pushed open a door to the outside. Cold spring air rushed over her skin and she welcomed the way it cleared her head even as goose bumps covered her arms.

An unused terrace ringed with a low stucco wall held outdoor couches and chairs. A few cast-iron sconces on the walls illuminated the space, but they seemed to flicker at half power.

"Here." He gestured toward a moss-colored love seat. "Will you be warm enough?"

He pulled his arm away now that they'd ditched the crowds. And no matter that it was wrong of her to notice, she felt a sharp pang of loss at the disappearance of his touch.

She couldn't remember ever feeling an attraction this tangible, let alone this ill-advised. Dropping into a cushioned chair, she planned to make sure they didn't touch again. She'd learned the hard way that a lack of objectivity with men could have devastating consequences. If her mom's relationships hadn't proven it—Marissa had never even met her birth father, a European tenor who'd fled the scene after a torrid affair with her mom—then her own experience should have sealed the deal. The one time she'd fallen head over heels, she'd been taken for a ride by a guy who'd only wanted to cash in on her mother's music industry connections.

That's why she preferred matchmaking others to romance for herself. All the fun of playing Cupid, none of the heartache. Besides, this way she helped other people avoid the mistakes she'd made. Her service ensured prospective daters looked beyond the physical.

"This is fine." The nip in the air would help keep her thoughts from overheating. She finally had Kyle Murphy all to herself. It was go-time to pitch her business. "I won't keep you for long—"

He waved away the concern as he took a seat on the cast-iron coffee table across from her. Removing his baseball cap, he tossed it on the couch nearby.

"I'll stick around the fundraiser late and meet with fans. It's not a problem. But I'll admit you've got me curious since you don't look like the kind of person to—you know—mess around behind someone's back."

It bothered her that he would think for a moment she was. He seemed to study her expression, as if he could gauge whether she had lied to him.

"I'm not." Before she could launch into her explanation, however, he continued.

"I guess that's a superficial judgment, though. Just because you dress like a sixties librarian doesn't mean you're necessarily the conservative type."

"Excuse me?" She straightened, her fingers clutching her shawl tighter to her shoulders.

"It's the clothes, I guess. Or maybe the glasses." He tipped his head sideways as if to get a better view. "You give off a buttoned-up vibe—"

"Like a Sixties librarian?" She tried not to be offended. She dressed modestly for a good reason. And she'd dressed sort of quirky her whole life since she wasn't a beautiful woman like her mom. Fitting into the superficial world of pop music hadn't really been an option for Marissa, so she'd deliberately chosen to be "interesting" instead of glamorous.

Her mom dressed for attention. Marissa dressed for deflection. Sometimes it was easier to be in costume than to show the world your true colors.

"I call 'em like I see 'em, but I'll admit I'm no fashion expert. So I'm going to shut up now and you can tell me what you wanted." He crossed his arms, as if he could rein in his commentary.

For a moment, she wondered if he'd get along with Stacy pretty well, after all. The arena heiress had a habit of speaking her mind, too. Maybe the pair would have something in common. And, of course, Stacy was stunning. Who wouldn't want a vivacious beauty?

"I'm a matchmaker," she blurted with renewed vigor for her mission. "That's why I wear the wedding band. It's helpful when I meet single men to take myself out of the equation since I look at them professionally and not personally. Although, maybe I don't need to bother with a ring if I come across as a buttoned-up librarian."

She hadn't meant to say that last bit out loud, but maybe his observation had stung a smidge even if it was probably accurate. Her one chance to convince Kyle to meet Stacy seemed to be going up in flames.

"You're *really* not married?" He seemed to key in on that fact, missing completely the rest of what she'd said.

"Never. But my point is that I wanted to speak to you from a professional perspective—"

"That's great." He touched her cheek with warm fingertips, smoothing along her skin in a slow sweep until he lifted her chin to meet his gaze in the electric glow of faux candle sconces.

"No, it isn't," she protested, scrambling to her feet. Away from the touch that distracted her completely. "I'm not here to talk about me. I—"

He rose, his big, athletic body straightening. His white shirt was bright next to his tanned skin. Damn it, she couldn't think when he came closer. She found herself staring at the column of his throat above his collar, his broad chest that loomed close enough to touch.

"It's okay. I believe you." He reached for her and she thought all was lost.

Heaven help her, she'd never pull herself together if he kissed her.

Thankfully, he did nothing of the sort. Instead, he took her left hand in his and drew the gold band off her finger. His touch was gentle. Slow. Deliberate.

When the ring was off, he rolled it between his thumb and forefinger, never releasing her. She peered up at him, to find him grinning, his teeth a flash of white in the moonlight.

"Then let's just get this out of the way." He pressed the ring into her palm and folded her hand around it. "No sense complicating things."

"Yes. Okay." When he finally relinquished her, she seemed to be able to think again. She backed up a step, only to find herself against one of the low stucco walls ringing the ground-floor terrace.

Kyle's eyes locked on hers.

"Looks like you're between a rock and a hard place, Marissa Collins."

NORMALLY, KYLE DIDN'T play games with women.

But the jumpy, jittery, delicious female in front of him had played one hell of a game on him with that ring. So he wasn't going to second-guess what he was about to do for payback.

"I—beg your pardon?" She pushed her glasses up higher on her nose and he could almost imagine her trying to resurrect that good-girl armor she wore.

Who was she beneath the carefully constructed facade?

"No need to beg." He edged closer, cornering her as

effectively as he checked opponents on the ice. "I'm at your service."

"Excellent." She feinted left and ducked right with shifty moves that surprised the hell out of him. Suddenly, she was behind him, and by the time he spun around to catch sight of her, she'd yanked that white silk shawl so tight around herself that her shoulders were effectively shrink-wrapped. "Then I would ask you to seriously consider my services, Mr. Murphy. As someone new to Philadelphia, I'm sure you'd enjoy the benefit of meeting a few nice girls without the hassle of trying to seek them out on your own. I'm sure you're a very busy man."

His pulse throbbed faster than normal and he realized it was out of frustration. Disappointment that he'd missed out on a kiss he'd really, really wanted.

"Are you honestly giving me a sales pitch?" Scrubbing a hand through his hair, he tried to get a handle on Marissa Collins. "Here? Now?"

"I'm not selling anything. And I apologize if the timing is less than ideal, but I assure you that I'm excellent at what I do. I work with men and women who are looking for that special someone—"

"I'm not looking for anyone special." He spread his arms wide and declared the point loud and clear to the world at large. "But I will tell you what I *am* looking for."

Lowering his arms, he reevaluated his approach to the cagey matchmaker who insisted on talking business when he had better things in mind. He calculated the best angle of pursuit and stalked toward her slowly. Carefully.

Because damn it, he hadn't been reading the signals that she'd been giving him wrong.

There was more at stake between them than a sales pitch.

"Mr. Murphy—"

"Kyle." He got closer without startling her.

"Kyle." She licked her lips, and he wondered if she liked the taste of his name there. "I represent some of the city's most beautiful, eligible women."

"I have no time for dating at this point in my career. And to be honest, I'm not interested in any matchmaking service right now whether or not I pay for it."

His summer would be spent setting up his youth hockey camp, in fact. He'd already talked to some potential sponsors for Full Strength Hockey Camp, a place where kids could learn the sport and gain confidence on the ice. Hockey was expensive and not everyone had the kind of support he'd had growing up. Seeing the kind of background his Finnish foster brother, Axel, had come from made Kyle want to give back. The world would have missed a great hockey player if Ax had been left to languish in Helsinki with a mom who'd already written him off.

So his short-term goals didn't include anything serious in the dating department. That didn't mean he couldn't cash in on a taste of Marissa Collins.

"You wouldn't," she assured him quickly, cutting him off. Her grip on her silk shawl loosened.

"Okay." He noticed she'd stuck the fake wedding band on the thumb of her right hand. Her short fingernails were neat and free of polish, as perfectly groomed as the rest of her. "This is really important to you, isn't it?"

"Finding the right person should be important to you, too." She dug in her purse and came up with a navy-blue linen business card with a local address.

"But you've sought me out for a reason." He didn't take the card. He had the feeling she'd bolt from the terrace the second she closed this deal. "And since I'm not paying you to locate potential candidates to hook up with, someone else must have a bounty out on me."

She straightened, her indignation wiping away the expression of polite, professional distance.

"I do not facilitate hookups, Kyle. My track record for arranging long-lasting, significant relationships speaks for itself."

"Then you can arrange an enduring relationship for another guy, okay? Not me." He'd followed her back to the center of the terrace near the low couch and chairs they'd first sat in.

While it was tempting to back her up to the coffee table and take that kiss his mouth was watering for, a better plan came to mind involving more finesse and less coercion. More of a give-and-go play as opposed to a hard-core slap shot.

Crumpling her business card in her hand, she studied him as if he was a particularly vexing opponent. The fact that she hadn't walked away yet spoke volumes about how much she wanted his cooperation. He'd all but insulted her business and he'd tried to corner her into a kiss. It wasn't one of his finer moments, but she'd caught him off guard at every turn.

"Unless…"

He let the word dangle between them, the carrot he needed to entice her.

"What?" She halted the idle mangling of her business card.

"Maybe we could work a trade."

"I don't follow you." She shook her head, a furrow creasing the creamy skin of her forehead.

"Let's say that I agree to one date with this client of yours who has a hankering to meet me." He knew that had to be the case. She wouldn't have pursued him this hard unless someone has specifically requested him.

Did she owe that client a favor or need to impress that person for some reason?

"You'd want something in return." Her gaze narrowed behind the heavy tortoiseshell frames. "Something beyond the obvious benefit of a pre-screened, beautiful, intelligent date."

"Since we've already established that I don't see that as a benefit to me, I think it's only fair I receive some other advantage."

"Unconventional. But I'm listening." Her tone was all business.

"In exchange, you have to arrange a date of my choosing."

She waited a beat, as if looking for the catch.

"That can easily be arranged, of course," she agreed finally, the genial cooperative note in her voice a surefire indication that she was pleased with the deal. "Orchestrating dates is my specialty."

"With you." As he let the words sink in, he caved to the impulse to touch her. Hand settling on her forearm, he made sure she understood. "My price is a date with you, Marissa."

Her mouth opened. Snapped shut. The surprise in her eyes morphed into worry so fast he almost missed it. But then, her spine straightened and determination lit her expression.

"Impossible. That would be completely unethical."

He rolled his shoulders in a shrug—he couldn't show his disappointment or else he'd risk giving her too much power. Like getting a good deal on a car, you had to know when to walk away. But putting off the kiss he wanted wouldn't be easy. Especially not when they were alone out here under the stars. He stood inches from her and her chest rose and fell rapidly under the dark fabric of her dress. He'd bet anything he could take the kiss now and she wouldn't object.

At least not at first.

On second thought, this was the better plan. Hold out for the date that would lead to the kind of kiss he really had in mind. One where Marissa wouldn't come to her senses for hours. Days, maybe.

"Okay. If you change your mind, you can always ask for me at the Phantoms' practice rink. We're there every morning except Sundays unless the team is on the road."

He watched her a second longer, trying to read her expression. Then, with more effort than it took to battle through a penalty kill at the end of a long shift on the ice, Kyle turned and walked away.

3

"WHERE THE HELL HAVE you been, Murph?" Finnish defenseman Akseli Rankinen slugged Kyle in the shoulder to punctuate the question. "You've been MIA half the night."

Stationed along the back wall of the atrium behind the row of autographing tables, Kyle signed a vintage Phantoms jersey as the fundraising event came to a close. Lights came up in the conference center and his teammates squeezed in a few final autographs.

Akseli—shortened to Axel Rankin early in his career—seemed to be done with his signing obligations. He held his BlackBerry in one hand while his other massive palm boxed Kyle's shoulders. The player had lived with Kyle's family for his last year in high school to ease his transition into the NHL, so the friendship went deep. The Murphys had become a foster family for the Finnish transplant, giving him a home away from home after being raised in a rough neighborhood in Helsinki. Axel had been part of the trade to Philly in a package deal three weeks prior, but no matter what their future professional lives brought, they were brothers in every way that counted. Which meant Kyle wasn't about to share details on Marissa. Axel would have a field day if he knew Kyle was a wanted commodity for a matchmaker.

Ax might be his inspiration for the Full Strength Hockey Camp, but that didn't mean he'd let his brother give him a hard time.

"I had to school the bartenders on mixing drinks, remember?" He returned the jersey to a longtime fan, flattered the guy had wanted him to autograph alongside signatures he'd collected from some hockey greats over the past three decades. "I worked the bar for a while."

He might have gotten away with the excuse if the young backup goalie hadn't chimed in. A recent Russian import, the kid pointed a finger in Kyle's face.

"He go with girl." The goalie grinned as he threw him under the bus with a basic command of English they understood well enough.

All the other players hooted in a collective razz as the event planners began ushering out guests. Kyle waved over a few more fans anyhow, signing their programs at the last minute to make up for the time he'd been with Marissa. He hadn't seen her since she'd rejected his offer, though he'd kept a close eye on the crowd.

"Come on, Murph, you can't hide behind the fans forever," Axel called, slapping the Russian goalie on the back. "Since when are you distracted by the ladies during a play-off run?"

"Since never." He wouldn't jeopardize his focus on hockey; he'd worked too hard and his family had supported him too much to enable him to play at this level. Not many families would give their kid a season to play in a European youth league as a way to catch the eye of hockey scouts.

"I don't know about that," Leandre, the French-Canadian forward who played in the second line, piped up. His knuckles were still taped from a brawl on the ice two nights ago. "I saw the female in question. Great legs and a tight skirt. She had a naughty secretary thing going on with her hair all pinned up."

Kyle's grip on his pen tightened as he scrawled his signature on a souvenir-size hockey stick, two event programs and a bar napkin in quick succession. While he agreed with the other player's assessment, he sure as hell didn't appreciate the team's resident Casanova noticing Marissa. Finishing up the autographs, he gestured to the team gear around the tables.

"Are we going to yammer or load this stuff up for Coach?" He pulled out a box and started tossing in signs, flyers and magnets with the team schedule on it that they'd used for giveaways. "Last I knew, we signed up to volunteer and help out."

"Blonde or brunette?" Axel grabbed a box and went to work pulling down a team banner overhead, but he kept his BlackBerry in hand, obsessively checking for updates of a competitor's game in Tampa.

Kyle ignored him.

"Brunette. Sort of mysterious looking," the mouthy Canuck offered as he headed for the door, ditching on the event cleanup. "She hid behind sexy glasses."

"I'd hardly call it hiding," Kyle called as he shoved a pop-up display of the team's most famous players toward the Russian goalie to dismantle. "Besides, she wore a wedding ring. Did you notice or were you too busy checking out her glasses?"

Let them think she was already taken. Selfishly, he figured it would shut them up. Besides, Marissa hadn't seemed interested in dating so it wasn't as though he was scaring off potential admirers.

Although, maybe she simply hadn't been interested in dating *him*. The notion ticked him off.

"Dude, don't even tell me you left with a *married* chick." Axel stuffed his BlackBerry in his pocket, giving Kyle his undivided attention. Or perhaps he was just freeing up his hands in case a beat-down was in order.

Kyle knew Ax's code of honor wouldn't accept infidelity any more than he did. They shared more than family—they shared values that weren't always upheld by other pro athletes. Two players on the Phantoms were in the process of divorce this season thanks to philandering on the part of one partner or the other. So yeah, cheating was a sensitive issue. One of many reasons Kyle had no intention of getting involved with anyone right now.

"Of course not." Kyle realized his remaining teammates were staring at him. They'd forgotten the task of packing up. "She's a friend. We just needed to speak privately for a minute."

When no one moved, all intent on sticking their collective noses in his business, Kyle shoved away the box he was packing.

"I'm going to leave the rest to you guys since I did my share while you gossiped like a bunch of freaking teenage girls." He had better things to do than listen to overgrown pee-wee players dish about women.

Especially when the woman happened to be Marissa Collins.

He hadn't figured out his next move with her, but he was already regretting not taking her business card. He'd walked away, so he couldn't very well hunt her down now or he'd have to change his terms. And he really, really wanted that date.

The kiss.

Levering open a back door that led directly out onto the hotel's grounds, Kyle welcomed the night air in his lungs to cool the heat in his chest. He was frustrated with his teammates, sure. No guy wanted to see a ladies' man like Leandre Archambault salivate over a woman they were remotely interested in. But the greater fire in his veins came from the thwarted move he'd made on Marissa.

Just because he wasn't interested in pursuing a full-blown relationship didn't mean he wasn't plenty interested in pursuing…something simpler.

Taking the long way around to the parking lot gave him time to cool off and prevented him from having to deal with anyone else from the team. On his right, he noticed the low wall of the terrace where he'd spoken privately with Marissa an hour ago. Slowing his step, he saw the lights from the sconces still burned, but the patio was vacant now.

Had he really expected to see her?

He picked up his pace and jogged toward the valet stand to retrieve his car. He'd make a few discreet inquiries tomorrow to see what he could unearth about

Marissa. As the regular season came to an end, his days in Philly could be numbered if the Phantoms didn't make the play-offs. That sucked for all the usual reasons since he wanted to make his mark on this team and take them to the next level. But now he had a new reason for wanting to stick around Philadelphia, at least long enough to...

His feet skidded to a stop.

Because there, at the valet stand, stood Marissa. She still wore her sexy glasses and her silk wrap, her dark hair tucked in a neat twist. Only now, she was chatting away with Leandre Archambault, the teammate who'd thought she was so damn hot he'd catalogued everything about her in his description to the team less than ten minutes earlier.

A fierce wave of possessiveness rose up out of nowhere. He could totally appreciate why cavemen brandished a club to ward off their competition. In hockey, he could battle for what he wanted, but out here, he couldn't bodycheck his teammate into the boards or throw down gloves in the parking lot of a fancy hotel.

"Marissa." He hadn't meant to announce himself until he had a plan, but her name rolled off his lips unconsciously, a primal need to stake his claim.

Both heads turned. Marissa gave him a distant, polite smile that was a far cry from the fireworks he'd seen in her eyes earlier. Leandre presented a Cheshire cat grin that told him he'd been making a play for the sizzling-hot matchmaker.

"Can I give you a lift?" Kyle offered, urging her silently with his eyes. Didn't she recognize a player when she saw one?

"I have my car, thank you." She kept her chin high, no doubt enjoying her opportunity to rub his nose in the fact that he'd walked away from her before.

An awkward pause followed where Leandre seemed to be waiting for him to get lost and Kyle fought the urge to haul Marissa away to address the unfinished business between them.

Finally, Leandre spoke up. "Marissa is a professional matchmaker. I thought I might test out a new way of dating."

Kyle nearly choked on the guy's gall.

"You're kidding, right? Have you told her that your idea of a first date involves a hotel room? Or that you have about as much intention of committing as—"

"Okay." Marissa slid her hand around his forearm, her fingers spread wide like the talons on a bird of prey. "Enough. Did you have something to discuss with me, Mr. Murphy?"

"Damn right, I do."

"Hey, I was here first," Leandre whined until Marissa smiled serenely at him.

"And I'm so grateful that you're considering my offer, Mr. Archambault. May I give you a call tomorrow to follow up on our conversation?"

Leandre grinned like a kid playing teacher's pet, his smile so ingratiating and fake it was all Kyle could do not to snarl.

"I look forward to hearing from you." He acted as if he wanted to say more, but the valet rolled up with the guy's flashy black-on-black BMW X5. "I'm very interested."

As he slid into his car like a snake into its den, Marissa released her hold on Kyle's arm.

"What business did you want to discuss?" She turned on him, arms folded, her manner decidedly less pleasant under the harsh exterior lights surrounding the valet's key rack.

"I was trying to save you from that low-life."

"The only thing you accomplished was scaring off business and potentially harming my bottom line." Her violet-blue eyes gave no quarter, the unusual color vivid even through the glasses. "In a night when you've already cost me a bundle, how can you honestly deny me the chance to sign on some potential candidates for my services?"

"Is that what dating is all about these days?" He snagged his keys and handed them to one of the kids retrieving cars. "Fattening up your bottom line?"

MARISSA FELT AS THOUGH a pin had been stuck in the balloon of her frustration. All her righteous indignation at Kyle's he-man tactics hissed away as she deflated right there in the parking lot.

Kyle's words exposed a weakness she wasn't proud of, the fact that she might be selling out to help her mother. But, oh, God, what choice did she have?

"What's the matter?" he continued to rant, oblivious to the raw nerve he'd struck. "Cat got your tongue? Truth hurt?"

A snappy comeback was really called for right about now. She needed to deflect and march away. But she'd failed on every level tonight and she didn't have it in her to argue with a man who hadn't let her off the hook for her shortcomings.

"Actually, yes." She shoved her glasses higher on her nose, wishing she had a plastic barrier to shield the rest of her body from this man's appeal. "Perhaps you have struck too close to the truth for my liking." She cleared her throat to get rid of the frog that lurked there. "I will take your complaint under advisement."

Blindly, she reached for her keys on the valet stand, but they all looked alike to her, and for some reason, the display appeared blurry.

"Oh, crap." Suddenly, Kyle was right beside her, tilting her chin up in his big, broad palm, angling her face under the hideous fluorescent lights. "I made you cry."

The utter horror in his voice snapped her out of the momentary self-pity. Thankfully, her voice was steady.

"Don't be ridiculous," she chided, mustering all the cool disdain possible. "Spring is hay fever season. Something on the grounds has been making my eyes water all night."

"Do I look like I was born yesterday?" He held his hands away from his body and stepped back, as if to give her an unimpeded view.

She wanted to laugh, her emotions boiling over after a day from hell. No, a year from hell. But no matter that he was being irreverent, her gaze raked over him from head to toe, lingering in the middle. Heat flared inside her as she responded the way any red-blooded woman might to an invitation to ogle a man who looked like him.

"Um. No." Her grip tightened on her shawl, her arms

hiding her body's reaction to him. "You look full grown to me."

The throaty hitch in her voice couldn't have sounded more sexually aggressive if she tried. But damn it, she *hadn't* tried. She just felt inexplicably attracted to him and that scared her.

"Your car's ready, sir," a young valet informed them from behind Kyle. She hadn't heard Kyle request his car—the kid must have just recognized him and brought the automobile around.

The teen must have been there for a while as he'd already vacated the driver's seat of the midnight-blue Audi coupe. Now he held the passenger side door open, as if he fully expected Marissa to get into the car with Kyle.

Her excuse hovered on her lips.

But the sexy hockey god shut it down by darting in with a precisely aimed kiss that sealed in the words.

It was more functional than anything, but that didn't stop her heart from leaping into overdrive in her chest. Before she even had the chance to process what had happened, his lips were beside her ear, whispering softly into her hair.

"The night is young. We'll go for a quick drive and I'll have you back in an hour, safe and sound."

She seriously doubted she'd be any more "sound" after spending time with a man who scrambled her thoughts and made her pulse race. But the night had done a number on her. The pressure had built to such a boiling point with her mom that she didn't know where to go next to afford the medicine she needed. And in order to snag the man she'd promised Stacy, Marissa would have to beat out the competition.

"Come on," he urged, his lower lip grazing her cheekbone in a caress that kicked off a hum of awareness deep inside her. "I think you'd agree we have some unfinished business between us."

Easing back from him, she found his steady gaze on her and realized she couldn't even look away, let alone walk away. She had no idea if the unfinished business he referred to had to do with her matchmaking proposition or the heat sizzling along her skin. Right now, she wasn't sure she cared.

With an unsteady nod, she agreed to his terms and headed for his car.

4

IN THE PARKING LOT OF THE Normandy Farm Hotel, Stacy Goodwell tried to say good-night to the man stuck to her like glue.

"Thank you for offering to walk me to my car." She stepped back from the overeager concert promoter she'd danced with earlier tonight and promptly caught her heel in a crack between the pavers. She stifled a wince. "But I'll be fine from here."

"Are you sure?" He reached to steady her and looked skeptical about her ability to navigate the parking area.

"Absolutely." She danced away again and gave him a friendly wave. "Good night."

Blake had seemed harmless enough at first. But she was a wretched judge of people. It had been proven many times in a colorful dating career that included a charming thief who'd stolen all her jewelry and an in-the-closet gay man who'd only wanted her as a smoke screen for his disapproving parents. True to form, Blake had gone from fun to pushy about twenty minutes ago and Stacy was stuck trying to send him on his way.

In some ways, she didn't blame her father for wanting to help her find a great guy through a matchmaking service. She could honestly see his point. On the other hand, how could she look at herself in the mirror if she allowed her *father* to pick the men she dated? The idea was ludicrous. But telling that to her dad was even tougher than shaking her clutching escort.

Initially, she'd hoped that setting her sights on an impossible date request in the form of hockey star Kyle Murphy would buy her time until she figured out what to do next. Sort of a passive-aggressive rebellion. She hadn't counted on her father being on board with the plan—micromanaging the process and bullying her into attending the fundraiser tonight. In hindsight, she realized the idea of her landing a socially acknowledged great catch had appealed to his competitive side, which was legendary. He'd made Kyle Murphy a personal mission.

What a mess.

"What kind of gentleman would I be if I left a lady alone out here?" Blake Someone-or-other caught up to her and gave her a knowing you'll-be-mine-soon look that set her teeth on edge. The diamond studs in his eyebrow winked in the light of a streetlamp.

It was a flaw of her character that she couldn't just tell guys like this to buzz off. For one thing, she expressed herself better in writing, where she had time to think and formulate her ideas. She loved her job with the local paper even though her dad considered it a waste of time. For another thing, she was a confirmed people-pleaser and preferred to coast along without making waves. She was the queen of disappearing after a trip to the ladies' room.

But Blake Whoever was proving tough to shake. Where was Marissa Collins to run interference?

"Actually," Stacy improvised, her feet killing her in the new stilettos that had pinched her heels even before she'd twisted her ankle. "My matchmaker insists I don't start any relationships unless she's involved. She already spoke to me tonight about agreeing to dance with you without—you know—following proper procedure."

A flimsy excuse or a stroke of genius? She'd realized early on that Blake had only been hitting on her because of her wealthy father. Concert promoters liked to cozy up to the folks who owned big arenas, the same way her father hoped to woo business from the Murphy family if Stacy dated Kyle.

"You have a matchmaker?" He raised his diamond-studded brow.

"A strict one, unfortunately. My father insisted on it." She extricated her arm from his hand and hated herself for playing the "dad" card. How would she assert her independence when she still relied on the family clout? "If you'd like, you can catch her in the lobby. Her name is Marissa."

Putting her feet in high gear, she took advantage of her escort's hesitation and hurried away as fast as her tyrannical shoes would allow. Weaving around a commercial truck, she never looked back, stopping only when she arrived at her base model American-made minivan. She'd bought the used silver Dodge Grand Caravan after her father berated her for wrecking the new Jaguar he'd bought for her twenty-first birthday. She'd only just gotten her license at twenty-one, after years of being chauffeured at his insistence. Who gave a new driver an expensive foreign car as a first vehicle? He'd been so mad about the wreck, he hadn't dared yell more when she'd replaced the ride herself with money earned working for the local paper.

She dropped her keys twice and hurried to put the right one in the lock. Was it upside down? The fit seemed tight.

Come on.

Peering toward where she'd left Blake the Snake, she jammed the key in again and twisted hard.

"Are you trying to wreck my van on purpose?"

A male voice behind her startled her into a partial coronary and she jumped backward half a foot. A rumpled, grouchy-looking man wearing a faded Phantoms T-shirt glared at her. Thick, dark hair curled around his forehead and stood straight up in the middle as if he'd recently tried to pull it out. Low slung jeans revealed a good body, if a little underfed. Dark heavy eyebrows needed waxing about a decade ago. He carried a rolled up poster under one arm, probably fan paraphernalia from the hockey team's fundraiser.

"Excuse me?" Her heart beat fast as she realized how isolated they were. The doorman seemed a million miles away and her touchy-feeling former dancing partner must have given up.

The man bent to retrieve her keys, which she'd dropped when he'd scared her to death. They were at least four feet away and half under the vehicle in front of hers.

"I wanted to know if you're trying to break into my van or if you're just doing your damnedest to scratch the paint." He handed over the keys and dropped them into her palm, careful not to touch her.

The gesture was so remote and aloof that she felt both grateful he didn't crowd her and miffed that he'd made such a production of not touching her. A silly thought, obviously.

"Your van?" She scrutinized the vehicle. The gray cloth interior was just as she remembered.

"Yes. Mine." His gaze narrowed. "Have you been drinking?"

"Of course not." She tried to put her key in the lock again.

"Would you like me to call you a cab?"

"I'll be fine, thanks." Flipping the key, she tested the lock in vain and got a sinking feeling in her stomach.

This wasn't her van.

"Why don't you try this one?"

Turning to face him, he held out his set—two keys on a plain silver fob, a far cry from her set of seven on a ring stuffed full of charms, including a stuffed leopard that helped her find them in her purse.

"I must have made a mistake," she admitted, feeling oddly foolish. She did things like this all the time, so it wasn't as though she had a problem being in the wrong. She'd accepted her lack of grace long ago—about the same time she'd realized men had tunnel vision when it came to women. Guys who were staring at your cleavage didn't notice when you tripped over your feet.

Yet the stranger in the Phantoms shirt didn't seem distracted by her cleavage. He zeroed in on her eyes in the dim light of the parking lot and seemed to see straight through her.

"Do you drive a Caravan?" he asked, not glaring anymore.

"Yes." Pivoting, she stretched up on her toes to see around the lot. Where the heck had she parked?

And why did the guy in the Phantoms' shirt make her feel so suddenly naked when he didn't look at her with even the tiniest bit of male interest?

"I have to say I'm surprised."

"Excuse me?"

"You don't look like you belong in a minivan."

"I love my Caravan," she said fiercely, probably because her choice in cars had been questioned by her dad more than once. As she shifted her weight, her feet protested how long she'd spent on the tarmac.

"Me, too. Can I give you a lift to help you find yours?" He edged past her cautiously, giving her plenty of personal space until he took her place in front of the driver's-side door. "You look like your feet hurt."

How had he noticed when he hadn't looked anywhere but her eyes?

"I—um. They do. But I'd better not." In a conversation full of surprises, she realized she'd had no problem telling him "no." Maybe because she knew it wouldn't disappoint him, unlike the guys who tried hard to catch her attention.

"Right. Probably best not to take a ride from a stranger. But I'm sure hotel security has a car. They can help you find your van." He opened the door easily and shoved the poster he'd been carrying inside. "I think you're going to need them because there are no other silver Caravans nearby."

"How do you know?" She craned her neck again.

"I make it a point to know my surroundings at all times." He extended his hand. "Isaac Reynolds."

"Stacy Goodwell." Tentatively, she accepted the handshake. "I'm sorry if I've scratched your paint."

Warm strength surrounded her fingers as he gave her hand a friendly squeeze. Gentle, but competent. She couldn't remember caring one way or another about a handshake before, but she liked the feel of Isaac.

"I have touch-up paint at home. I'm sure it will be fine." He released her fingers long before anyone could ever accuse him of flirting with her.

Maybe that was the problem. She didn't know quite how to relate to a man who showed utterly no interest in her. She was confounded. And, perhaps, charmed because of it.

"On second thought." Why should she fear a man who was in a hurry to go home and put touch-up paint on his van? She had mace in her purse if her instincts were wrong. "I'd actually appreciate some help finding my vehicle. Would you mind walking down the row with me?"

As flirtation attempts went, it wasn't much. But she didn't have any experience on this side of the equation. She'd been pursued so often, she'd never had to do the chasing.

And considering a pressing need to figure out her love life before her father contracted away her rights to it, Stacy liked the idea of making a move on Isaac Reynolds.

For a moment, he studied her with what almost looked like suspicion in his eyes. But that was crazy. Suspicious of what?

"I can do that," he agreed, nodding.

She must have imagined his hesitation.

Following him with a new spring in her step, she could almost forget about the relentless clench of her shoes on her heels. Until a stone on the pavement made her turn her ankle. Sending her right into Isaac's arms.

"I'M SURE YOU'RE NOT a sellout." Kyle regretted his earlier accusation after seeing how much it affected Marissa. "I have a bad habit of saying whatever comes to mind without thinking it through."

They drove around his Chestnut Hill neighborhood since it was one of the few areas of Philadelphia that he knew. He'd only been in town for a few weeks and with his team in the play-offs, hockey had consumed every second of his time. But Marissa didn't seem to care where they were going, her eyes fixed out the front windshield, her gaze a million miles away.

"Being spontaneous doesn't make it false." She tugged off her glasses and folded them up, tucking them into a small evening bag. At the same time, she pulled a folded newspaper page from her purse. "And I knew about your tendency to speak your mind. I thought that would give you and Stacy a common trait. But I realize now that she tends to comment on more irreverent topics that feel like they come out of nowhere, while you cut to the chase."

"Sounds like there would be a huge lack of impulse control in a relationship like that," he observed, turning down the street where Axel had bought a house. "We'd probably kill each other in a week."

"So tell me what you think would make for a good

relationship for you. I'm not asking to try to find you a date. I'd just like to know how I went wrong since I'm usually good at this kind of thing." She smoothed the folded newspaper clipping and he recognized the headline from yesterday's sports section. "All I know for sure is that you're great at scoring shoot-out goals."

He tucked into a dead-end street with an outlet onto a vast park. Technically, it was probably closed, but houses backed up to the public property for miles, and it wasn't fenced. He parked there and cut the headlights. Surrounded by maple trees full of new spring leaves, he cracked the window to catch the breeze.

"Well, you know the most important stuff." Glancing at the paper she held, he imagined her carefully cutting out the story and folding it into neat sections. He enjoyed the idea of her carrying around his picture, even if it had been for business. "I grew up on Cape Cod. I have five brothers, four by blood and one because I picked him."

Even Kyle didn't know the full story about Axel's past, but he'd urged his family to foster Ax in the U.S. because the guy had gotten into trouble with a bad crowd while he was in high school. But he was aces on the ice.

"How does one go about picking a brother?" She swiveled toward him in her seat and he was mesmerized by the unobstructed view of her gorgeous eyes.

"Axel and I played on an international junior team together. From day one, he told me that if I scored the goals, he'd make sure no one got in my way."

"He sounds sure of himself."

"He talks smack but he backs it up. The guy cleaned

up the ice with the competition. He was like a Murphy separated at birth." Kyle hadn't realized how effective they worked as a team until they'd been reunited this year, each of them experiencing record-breaking seasons. "Ax wanted to come to the U.S. for a better shot at making it in the NHL, so I hounded my mom and dad to take him in."

"You must have great parents." Tucking the newspaper back into her bag where it lay on the console between them, she was ready to snap the purse closed when he noticed the decoy wedding ring inside.

With the lightning-fast hands that allowed him to compete at the highest level of his sport, Kyle reached in the bag to filch it.

"You must not date enough if you're wearing a wedding ring every time you go out." Rolling the band between his thumb and forefinger, he held it up to one eye like a monocle.

Too bad it didn't really work to bring this mysterious woman into better focus.

"You said you have no time for dating right now, either, so I'm not alone in putting my career first," she said carefully.

He had to admire how easily she'd turned that one around.

"So we agree seeing people isn't a good idea because we're too busy." He lowered the ring and slid it back into her bag, not wanting to see it on her finger.

She frowned. "I still believe you would benefit from expanding your horizons."

"And I think going out with me would be great for you." He shifted closer, leaning one arm into the console where her fingers rested. "You see how I have you cornered? Any argument you make for *me* dating is only going to be an argument I'll make for *you* to date me."

"That's not logical." She angled forward, too, so she could argue with him; whereas he was leaning forward in order to kiss her. "If you don't have time to be matched with a woman, you wouldn't have time for me."

"There's always time for the things in life that are most important."

"You don't even know me," she protested, her tone conveying a large dose of exasperation that he felt only a little guilty about. Her violet eyes sucked him in and made him want to linger in the spotlight of that gaze.

"I know you a whole hell of a lot better than I know the Ms. Anonymous who wants to go out with me." He'd been attracted to Marissa from the moment she ordered a shot of Scotch with her Coke. She was an original from head to toe, oddly unassuming and obviously comfortable on the sidelines, but that was exactly why he wanted to be with her. A woman like that would never date someone just for fame and fortune. "It would be hypocritical of me to date someone else when I'm really, insanely attracted to *you*."

Watching her, he let the heat build all around them without saying a word. Without moving an inch. He didn't need to. The magnetism simply existed, as surely as a scientific principle, whether or not they acted on it.

Slowly, she shook her head. "I can't. What kind of matchmaker would I be if I swooped in and took the prize catch for myself? No client would ever trust me again."

Her voice, so impossibly soft, was the only hint that her resolve might have weakened. She sat utterly still, caught in the same heat wave as him, but she seemed determined to ignore it.

"So stubborn," he observed, taking her hand in his to stroke the backs of her fingers. Trace the rise and fall of her knuckles where her skin was smooth and creamy. "But who would trust you if you set me up with someone else and, in the meantime, you and I couldn't keep our eyes off each other?"

A breeze drifted in through the window and Marissa lifted her chin as if to catch the cool air on her face. He had the feeling she was trying to find the will to tell him off and shut things down between them. So, upping his game, he raised a finger to her upturned face and sketched a soft stroke down the length of her throat.

Her eyelids fluttered. Her lips parted. And he would have had to have been superhuman to resist the way she looked right then.

"Marissa." Her whispered name was the last warning he intended to give. Even that was more invitation than anything.

Skimming a touch behind her neck, he drew her closer. His pulse revved as if he'd been running a speed workout as he imagined taking down her hair and letting it spill all over his hands. He caught the floral and spicy scent of her, something exotic and sexy but so slight he'd have to really inhale to identify it.

His lips hovered over hers as he savored the moment and the woman. At the last minute, though, she hooked her fingers over his shoulders and pulled him into her, taking the kiss.

Her mouth was slick with lip gloss and cinnamon flavor, a surprisingly girlish touch on a woman who worked hard to deflect attention. He wanted to lick and nibble away at the flavor until he'd uncovered the woman beneath. Hunger surged after being reined in all night, and he battled to keep the kiss light and seductive. This could not be a one-time deal.

Suppressing the urge to let his hands roam freely, to explore her slight curves, he distracted himself by tugging pins out of her hair. One. Two. Three.

The shiny mass tumbled down to her shoulders, releasing the scent of citrus. Her hair was so thick it was still damp in some places, as if she'd washed it before she went to the fundraiser. He combed his fingers through, unable to get enough of her. He wanted to taste her, touch her, breathe her in. Lips traveling down her neck, he sought the source of her scent while he savored her creamy skin. Spearing his fingers deeper into her hair, he cradled the base of her skull, angling her this way and that until he found the hint of scent behind one ear. Orchids maybe. Or some extravagant night-blooming flower.

Inhaling deeply, he rubbed his cheek there, bathing in a fragrance he knew he'd never forget.

If not for the constraints of the car, he would have been all over her. No. He would have pulled her on top of him, pressed her against him. He didn't know whether to curse the damn console or be grateful for the restraint it imposed.

"What are we doing?" she whispered helplessly

against his ear, her fingers clutching his shoulders as if she was hanging on for dear life.

The image pleased the hell out of him. "Being impulsive." He licked his way into the curve of her shoulder and felt her shiver. "Isn't it the best?"

Liking her reaction, he ran his tongue along that same spot over and over again until she trembled again.

"I'm not impulsive." She said it even as she arched her neck to give him more room to work.

"You are now." He wanted to press her back into the leather seat and see if he could make her whole body shudder. But he wouldn't taint that victory with the knowledge that he'd pushed his luck on a night that had been tough on her.

A night where he'd made her cry.

His conscience kicked in then, reminding him that he needed to play fair.

With more than a little regret, he eased back, breaking away in slow degrees since he didn't think he could quit touching her completely. She blinked up at him, passion-dazed and breathing fast.

Exactly what he wanted and yet precisely why he needed to take a break. He'd be willing to bet that, under normal circumstances, she would have battled the attraction more.

But something upset her tonight and he had the feeling there was more to it than just him.

"You're realizing we made a huge mistake." She released her hold on his shoulders, her hands sliding away to fold neatly in her lap. "I agree."

"No. Hell, no." He took in the sight of her with her hair down and tousled around her shoulders, liking the idea that he'd been the only one to see her this way tonight. "I just didn't want to push my luck, and I knew if I didn't quit soon…there would have been no stopping."

As it stood—and wasn't that an apt expression considering his current condition?—Marissa would be a fixture in his dreams, most certainly at the cost of sleep.

All of which would be a detriment to his practice tomorrow, but he couldn't bring himself to care right now.

"That was thoughtful of you." She picked up a pen from the change tray in the console. "May I borrow this?"

"Sure." He shrugged, wondering what she could want to write at a time like this. "I don't have any paper."

"That's okay." Gathering her hair, she twisted and rolled the dark strands and then jammed the pen down into the center of the roll, magically keeping the whole thing in place. "I should be getting back to my car."

She studied him in the dim light of the half-moon and a streetlamp behind his car. Then, like a lady warrior who hadn't finished putting on her armor, she retrieved her glasses from her purse and slid them into place on her nose.

Kyle ran a finger along the top of the frames.

"You might as well put a tissue between us for all the good those do."

"The more barriers the better." She dug into her handbag again.

"What else do you have in there? A false nose? A

burka?" How much more could she distance herself from him? Would he ever have a shot at being with her again or had he already seen as much impulsiveness as she possessed?

She withdrew a folded sheet of paper and handed it to him.

"No. Something else guaranteed to send you running."

Frowning, he unfolded the heavy stock and saw the fine print of a detailed questionnaire about his dating preferences. It was a matchmaking form, probably standard issue for her clients.

"After what just happened, you're giving me this?" He'd taken shots to the jaw that had had less impact. "You can't be serious."

All traces of the violet-eyed temptress were gone. She straightened in her seat and smoothed her skirt.

"Just in case you change your mind."

5

MARISSA RETURNED HOME after midnight, her headache now outweighed by a heartache so complex she couldn't quite put a name to it. Regret, guilt, sexual frustration…a mixed bag of negative emotions she wished she could lock down and forget about.

Quietly, she opened the back door to her mother's house in west Philly, not all that far from where Kyle had driven her around Chestnut Hill. She had liked being with him. Even before the kissing, she'd enjoyed sitting beside him in his car. He'd taken her for a ride because he'd upset her, a small gesture she'd found endearing.

Then, the kissing had been transporting. There was no other word for the way his touches had inflamed her until she'd been ready to leap across the console and straddle him. She'd been out of her mind for him while he'd been controlled and composed, pulling away so that he wouldn't take advantage of her mindlessness, apparently.

How mortifying. It had been all she could do to restore order to her hair, let alone resurrect any semblance of pride. Shoving that damn dating questionnaire in his face had been a last-minute attempt to resurrect some boundaries. Self-respect.

Maybe she ought to be dating, after all. Who knew she was so affection-starved that she'd wrap herself around Kyle like a boa constrictor in search of a meal? Perhaps she should try to be objective about making a match for herself. Look for a candidate on paper where all the attractive intangibles didn't get in the way and cloud her judgment....

"Marissa?" a frail voice called from the dining room, which they'd converted into a bedroom after her mother's accident. "What are you doing out of bed, young lady?"

Regretting whatever noise she'd made to disturb her mother, Marissa set her keys on a kitchen counter and stepped out of her shoes before pushing open the swinging door to the dining area in the turn-of-the-century mansion. She nodded to her mother's caregiver, relieving her from duty.

Surrounded by glossy mahogany paneling that rose three-quarters of the way up the walls, a queen-size bed sat illuminated by a reading light clipped to the headboard. Marissa had lined the walls with guitars and sequined stage costumes in an effort to help her mother remember who she was on a daily basis; a décor built on remnants of a life fragmented by the traumatic brain injury resulting from the late-night car crash when Brandy's agent had flipped her convertible. Those reminders were one reason Marissa had worked so hard to keep the house for her mother, selling off anything and everything else to maintain consistency in Brandy's life so that nothing would upset her while she healed.

At the center of all the memorabilia sat Brandy Collins, her glossy dark hair missing patches in front from a surgery to slow down swelling in her brain. Her face remained as lovely as ever. If anything, the medications that sedated her had relaxed the animated age lines around her eyes and mouth, making her appear younger. On the wall behind her, a poster from a concert ten years ago showed her as she used to be—clad in black leather, head thrown back as she belted out a song with an angel's voice that hadn't been handed down in the DNA code to her daughter.

As exasperating as Brandy used to be at times, Marissa missed her passion. Her zest for life.

"I'm fine, Mom." Marissa sidestepped a table with a jigsaw puzzle and photo albums, more tools in a recovery that had shown little progress in the past six months. "Just getting a drink of water."

Marissa never knew if her mother would address her as an adult, a teenager, or a five-year-old. Some days she cycled through all three, as if she'd stepped into a time machine and made random stops along the journey of their lives together. But that was normal for traumatic brain injury patients, where the patient's life was affected in myriad ways. Some people lost the capacity for speech or lost all their memories. Sometimes people lost motor coordination, or their personalities were completely altered. Doctors assured Marissa that they wouldn't know how extensive the damage would be until the brain's swelling had gone down completely and cerebral blood flow had returned to a regular pattern.

"You shouldn't have eaten so much cotton candy at the VIP party," Brandy fretted, dredging up some long-ago memory. "I knew I should have hired a sitter instead of letting you come with me."

Settling on the bed beside her, Marissa noticed her mother held a magazine upside down, her gaze glassy and unfocused. Gently, Marissa righted the glossy periodical—an old issue of *Vogue*.

"But I had the best time. Thank you for letting me go to the party." She played along whenever possible, trying not to add any details that might conflict with her mother's memories and agitate her more. The doctors all insisted it was best to keep her peaceful while her brain struggled to heal itself.

"You're welcome, princess." Smiling the dazzling grin that had made her a video queen back when MTV reigned supreme, Brandy Collins patted her daughter's head. "Off to bed now. Mommy has an early rehearsal."

On impulse, Marissa hugged her, soaking up all the maternal affection she could on a rare night when she really, really needed it. Kyle's suggestion that she'd sold out had bothered her, probably because it resonated with her own fears.

She didn't want to match up people who didn't belong together. And she sure didn't want to set up Kyle with Stacy after a kiss that had knocked her off her moorings. But without a payday in sight, how would she help mother? She hoped Kyle's teammate, Leandre, would sign on as a client. He'd confided that he was tired of his ladies' man reputation and ready for something more serious. She could really help him.

But without the bonus Phil Goodwell had offered her for matching up his daughter with Kyle…even a new client wouldn't make up the difference she needed for her mother's new medicine.

"Good night, Mom."

Pressing a kiss to her cheek, Marissa left the dining room to think up a plan. Selling the house or anything else from her mom's past was out of the question since those familiar items grounded her when she was confused. And with those assets off-limits, what choice did she have but to find another way to make her matchmaking service work? Only this time, she'd restrict herself to pairing people who *both* really wanted to find true love.

Which meant she needed to speak with Stacy Goodwell and tell her the news.

Pausing at the turn of the stairs to fish her cell phone from her purse, Marissa dropped into the deep cushions of the window seat tucked on the landing. She'd sleep better tonight if she sent Stacy a message and got it over with.

Tomorrow, she'd worry about finding new clients. *Multiple* new clients. For now, she clicked out a message.

I'm bowing out of the race to land Kyle Murphy. If you're interested in other options, I'd be happy to help you.

Jamming a finger on the send button before she could change her mind, Marissa opened her purse to put the phone back. The newspaper article with Kyle's picture fell out so that he seemed to be grinning at her even now.

Even if breaking her contract with Stacy cleared the path for Marissa to see Kyle, she still didn't trust the way she felt about him. That crazy, upside-down attraction could never be a good thing. At very least, it impaired her romantic judgment.

What if she was just another conquest to him, forbidden fruit his über-competitive side couldn't resist trying?

"I knew you'd be trouble," she whispered, stabbing the paper with an accusatory finger. "And I was right."

THE DAY HAD STARTED out like any other for Isaac Reynolds.

Ten hours at the office of his tech company messing with a top-secret idea for new 3-D technology for his graphics chip, an hour at the gym and a half hour supporting a worthwhile cause in the form of a fat check written to the charities the Phantoms hockey team supported.

A normal day for a successful geek trying to get a new product to market. Or it had been normal until now, when Isaac found himself with an armful of lush female who was light-years out of his league.

There's no way a woman like this fell into his arms unless she was an industrial spy sent by his competition. He had a long track record as a bachelor that proved it.

"Are you okay?" He tried to steady her after she'd stumbled into him, but she winced in pain.

"I hurt my ankle." Her grip on his shoulders tightened.

A whole hell of a lot more than that tightened on his end of the equation as she hopped around on one foot, her hip grazing him in ways that even a lap dancer couldn't have dreamed up. Whether she was a spy or not, he wasn't immune.

"Hold still," he barked, clamping his hands around her waist like a vise in order to save his sanity.

And while that halted the teeth-grinding tease of the dance she'd been doing, it introduced his hands to an inviting new landscape that practically begged for exploration. It wasn't fair a woman who felt this good would work for the competition.

"I'm trying," she protested. "These shoes have been killing me, and I ripped open a blister when I twisted my ankle."

Her eyes were squeezed shut as if she was fending off pain, and her genuine hurt chased away his cynicism for the moment. He tried not to think about the sweet indent of her waist above the soft flare of her hips. It wasn't easy with his body still dogging him to cop another feel. She was pure fantasy material.

"Are you sure you don't want me to find hotel security?" He could pass her off to someone else.

"I can manage. That is, if you're still amenable to looking around the parking lot with me?"

He gritted his teeth at the thought of touching her again—a sweetly torturous thrill.

"Sure."

"Thank you." She blinked up at him so gratefully he felt like a low-life for fantasizing about her.

As he locked his van for safety, he was surprised she hadn't tried to talk her way into his vehicle. Not that he carried research development notes with him. But she didn't know that.

"Are you okay to walk on that foot or do you want me to...carry you?"

He looked over her short, strapless dress, already regretting the offer. She possessed an incredibly sexy body and the dress showed it off to mouthwatering advantage. Her platinum blond hair had an asymmetrical cut that made her look as though she'd walked out of a futuristic video game—a zombie-killing spaceship captain, maybe. A character you could only access deep into the game, late at night. And only if you were very, very talented with your hands.

"I'll be fine." She—Stacy—bit her lip, appearing entirely unsure of herself as she tested her tender ankle.

Stifling an inward curse, he sent a stern message to his hands not to get used to this. But he needed to help her if she was going to find her van. Decision made, he bent forward to slip an arm around her shoulders, bolstering her so she leaned into his side. He was careful not to hold her too close since he hadn't quite willed away his earlier reaction to her.

"Oh!" Gasping in surprise, she wrapped her arm around his waist and wriggled infernally near.

"Did I hurt you?" Sticking to the main aisle where the light was best, Isaac began a methodical scan of the rows, searching for her vehicle.

"No. I was just startled since you didn't give me a warning. You don't have much to say, do you?"

And wasn't *that* the beginning of the end of this parking lot relationship? Isaac had scared off more than a few women with qualities they'd diagnosed as everything from "inability to relate" to "freakish quietness." So interludes like this one would only happen to him if a woman literally fell into his lap, as this hapless, hot blonde seemed to have.

Or she'd been paid to seduce his secrets from him. Being with her would almost make it worth selling out.

"Not really." He needed to drop her off somewhere else, somewhere she *belonged,* because she sure as hell didn't have any business here, plastered to his side.

"Are you still mad about me wrecking your paint job? Is that why you don't talk to me?" She leaned forward to peer down another row of cars and her breasts strained against the fabric of her sparkly dress.

Or so he imagined, since he kept himself occupied not looking at her.

"I live in my head a lot," he explained, forcing himself to slow down even though he wanted to sprint. He figured he'd go with the obvious answer instead of trying to dress up the truth.

"What do you mean?" Her frown created the perfect pout, her lower lip full and glistening.

"I think too much. Half the time I don't hear what people say, and the other half of the time, I'll think I've answered them when I haven't." Although he'd been shockingly tuned into her since he'd discovered her trying to break into his van.

He couldn't remember the last time a woman had so thoroughly claimed his attention.

"I wish the people in my life wouldn't hear half of what I say. Fifty percent of the time I haven't thought it out and wish I could take it back." She brightened, pearly white teeth as perfect as the rest of her. "Now that I think about it, we'd make the perfect couple."

"Ah. I see what you mean." He shook his head and paused to take in the shape of a minivan at the end of one aisle but realized the rear window was too sloped to be a Caravan.

The parking lot was thinning rapidly, but he still didn't see another vehicle like his in front of them so he steered around to the back to search there.

"You do?" she said, surprised and—oddly—a little breathless.

Isaac peered over at her and was taken aback by the warmth in her eyes. Could he be reading that right? A man could lose himself in that clear blue gaze of hers. For a moment, he wasn't sure what she was talking about and he had to run back through the conversation.

"You said you wished people would ignore half of what you say, then proved your point by suggesting you and I would make a good couple." Clever illustration, that. "Point taken."

"Oh." Her voice hitched and she cleared it, her hold on him loosening. "Yeah. Okay. I think I see my van." She pointed toward another Caravan in the back row of the lot, far from where they'd started out. She pulled her cell phone from her bag with one hand and studied the screen.

Apparently, she'd finished conversing with him. Maybe he'd offended her when he said he didn't talk much.

Then again, why would someone sent to learn his secrets allow herself to be offended? Shouldn't she keep up her chatty patter to try to see him again? Talk her way into his house or his office? His bed?

He was bizarrely disappointed she didn't at least try. She was the most interesting thing to happen to him in months. But maybe she knew he wasn't fooled by her act. Had she really expected him to buy her story that she'd confused his vehicle for hers when she hadn't even tried to park in the same vicinity?

Isaac guided her down the row of cars to the van with fat rhinestones around the license plate. Yeah, no way she would mistake that girly grill for his.

"I can give you a hand getting in." He steadied her while she searched for her keys, feeling strangely guilty for her retreat into quietness.

He should be grateful that he was sending her on her way, damn it. Releasing her, he saw a glint of tears on one cheek. Did her foot hurt that much? She clutched the cell phone to her chest as she came up with the keys.

Maybe she'd realized how badly she'd bobbled the task of spying on him. Steeling himself for whatever sob story excuse she might concoct to go home with him, he simply pointed toward her keys and ignored the tears.

"Would you like me to open your van and start it up for you?" Now who was the chatty one?

"That's okay." Hobbling forward, she jingled a noisy assortment of keys and plastic cartoon characters, most of which were painted pink and covered in glitter. Then, unlocking her vehicle, he noticed a fairy air freshener swinging from the radio knob. And someone had modified the glove compartment so that every inch was covered in rhinestones. She'd taken a lot of time with the details in creating a cover as an ultra-feminine bombshell.

But even now that the door was open, she didn't move.

"You're all set." He prodded, memorizing her license plate so he could have his security team investigate her tomorrow.

"My matchmaker just quit," she blurted, swiping away the tears on her cheeks. "My father is going to use his own and try to buy a man for me."

Whatever ploy Isaac had been prepping for, it hadn't been that. A matchmaker?

Standing on one foot, she took off her shoe and planted her injured heel on the ground.

"Be careful," he warned. "There could be glass—"

"I don't need help." Stacy turned on him fiercely, pausing in her hobbled progress into her vehicle. "Doesn't he get that? I need to figure out who to trust on my own and if I make a mistake along the way, that's how I'll learn. Can I help it if I figure things out the hard way?"

She started hopping again, her breasts threatening to break free of the neckline a little more each time. But given how upset she seemed, he didn't take the same pleasure in the show.

"Can I—" He reached to help her again.

"No." Collapsing into the driver's seat, she tucked the skirt around her thighs. "I put myself on the line for the first time ever to ask a guy out tonight, and you thought it was so ludicrous an idea you didn't even take me seriously. Another hint that I suck at dating, I guess. But I'm not giving up."

Huh?

She started the van and hauled her door shut, leaving him to scratch his head. Whatever had just happened here, Stacy Goodwell didn't behave like any corporate spy he'd ever met.

Rolling down her window, she seemed to be gearing up to rant at him more but he beat her to the punch.

"You asked me out?" Funny, because he'd been specifically listening for a pitch like that, figuring it would confirm that she was after the plans for his new 3-D graphics chip.

But apparently, he'd missed it.

"I said we'd make the perfect couple," she retorted. "Remember? You don't listen enough and I talk too much. I thought it sounded perfect. As an added bonus, you don't stare down my dress and you haven't paid me a bunch of ridiculous compliments meant to get me into bed. And for some reason—maybe because you don't seem like you're trying to impress me—I don't feel intimidated to say what I think with you."

She tried to turn the car over, but since the engine was already running, it made a scraping, squealing sound.

"Stacy." He had zero experience with hysterical females since he'd never incited this much emotion from a woman outside of bed. He wasn't quite sure what to do next.

Could he have read the situation wrong? What if she wasn't a spy and she was just a very unusual beauty with an overprotective father and a matchmaker trying to call the shots?

"Sorry again about trying to break into your van."

Putting the transmission into drive, she kept her foot on the brake and met his gaze under the buzzing fluorescent glow of a street lamp. Her eye makeup had smudged under one eye. "Goodbye, Isaac Reynolds."

Tearing out of the lot, she left him shaking his head and wondering what had just happened. As spy missions went, she'd obviously failed. But on the off chance that she *hadn't* been sent to learn his company's secrets, it was he who'd messed up royally. No man with red blood in his veins and a few functional brain cells would let a woman like that get away.

A woman who might have been attracted to him.

The possibility blew his mind.

The only thing left to do was run a check on her and see what he found. Because if she wasn't working for the competition, Isaac had a new goal in life, the first that didn't have anything to do with his business model. He'd chase his sexy, futuristic spaceship captain all the way back to her home planet if he had to. He'd do whatever it took to get her back.

6

BLADES FLYING OVER THE ICE, Kyle Murphy deked two defensemen, protecting the puck as if it was his first-born. Beating the competition, he came face-to-face with the goalie, a rare one-on-one shot opportunity. An opportunity he excelled at creating. Lifting his stick, he faked a drive to the body, refired and…missed the goal all together.

For a moment, his teammates seemed too surprised to react. That shot was his bread and butter. The money shot.

Didn't matter that this was a practice. He practiced like he played, and he always made that frigging shot.

Curses streamed from his mouth, rare for him even though the practice arena was frequently filled with creative and functional swearing alike.

Behind him, the coach's whistle blew to end practice. Leandre Archambault had the audacity to clap him on the back.

"Tough shot, Murphy." He almost kept a straight face when he said it.

Bastard.

"Ignore him." Axel was in his face before Kyle could fire back something he'd regret.

The Finn dropped a heavy arm around Kyle's shoulders and steered him away from their teammates as they headed toward the tunnel to the locker rooms and workout facility.

A foul mood had dogged him ever since he and Marissa had exchanged a terse good-night when he'd dropped her off at her car yesterday. He'd hoped that a good hard practice this morning would take the edge off, but if anything, he felt fiercer than ever.

"I don't miss that shot," he told Ax, even though his foster brother knew it as well as he did. "Leandre isn't taking the starting position from me because of one missed goal. I'm not worried about him. But I don't know what the hell went wrong just now, and that..."

Scares the crap out of me.

He didn't finish the sentence because he didn't need to. Ax would understand because hockey was a language they spoke fluently. Hell, some sports writers had suggested they had a telepathic connection on the ice. Their shots to each other were as fluid as any in the game, since they had a sixth sense for where each other would be.

"What's wrong today?" Ax let go of him and pulled his helmet off. A dark red U-shaped scar on his cheek added to the intimidation factor of an already big guy.

The coaches were heading in now, the ice clear of everyone but them. Outside the glass boards, Kyle could see the rink was about half full of fans who'd come to see a Phantoms' practice. Too bad he'd put on such a crappy show.

Ax wanted to know what was wrong?

"Marissa Collins." His problem had a name. "The woman from the fundraiser."

"You're kidding me, right?" Circling Kyle on his skates, Axel gave his shoulder a light punch. "It's you who always said women complicate the game. I didn't buy into it until the last one cheated on me and I started to play like crap. Now?" He made a decisive sweep with his hand. "No women while we're in the play-offs. End of sentence."

"Yeah. That's the principle I'm working under, too." Although if Marissa had shown any inclination to take things further last night, he had the feeling his resolution would burn to ash in the face of the heat they generated.

"What do you mean?" Axel stopped, glowering. "You said she was married."

"She wears a wedding ring as a decoy because she's a professional matchmaker and she doesn't want to attract attention."

"Doesn't she know some guys hit on married women just for the hell of it?"

Unfortunately, they had a guy like that on the team.

"I'm not sure. Either way, nothing happened between us." Other than Marissa giving him a matchmaking questionnaire to fill out. The memory still ticked him off. "But I can't stop thinking about her."

"Interesting." Axel nodded toward the tunnel, where the fans were now clustered by the players' exit, hoping for autographs or the chance to say hello. "You played it safe with her, yet you're still paying the price for it today."

More like *she'd* played it safe with *him*. But the end result remained the same. His game sucked eggs and he needed to get on track before the next series in Pittsburgh. The Phantoms franchise hadn't brought him here to play the way he had this morning.

They halted their conversation as they reached the mouth of the tunnel, where fans could stand above them and reach down with programs to autograph. Mostly, on a practice day, they came to just shake hands or exchange a word. These were the hard-core fans, local die-hards or faraway supporters who'd made a trip to catch a couple of games and a practice. A few hockey groupies showed up every day, a handful of women who'd had a hard go of it in life and enjoyed the sense of family that a sports team offered.

Ax took as much time as Kyle did, shooting the breeze with some, signing pucks and flyers for others. When they finished, they trudged over the carpet on their skates toward the locker room.

"Maybe the rules don't apply to this woman," Axel observed, picking up where they'd left off their conversation.

"Marissa?" Axel had managed to get her in his head again just when he'd avoided thinking about her for at least five minutes.

"The matchmaker," he clarified, his round vowels still carrying the sound of Helsinki. "We know it kills your game to be with the wrong females. But maybe there are other women—the ones you're meant to be with—who mess with your head when you avoid the inevitable."

"You think I should break the No Women in Play-off Season rule?" Pausing outside the locker room with a big Phantoms logo on the double doors, Kyle wasn't entirely sure he could win over Marissa even if he caved.

"Well," Axel said, grinning, his new front tooth blending seamlessly with the rest after being knocked out in a game the week before. "You see how you play when you're *not* with her. I would take a chance and see if being with her straightens you out. So to speak."

The Finn was surprisingly gifted in the double entendre for a foreign dude, but then, he'd been around a lot of smack-talking, innuendo-loving, crude conversationalists in U.S. hockey clubs.

Then again, he probably learned everything he knew from living with five brothers in the Murphy household.

"What if that doesn't help? What if being with her makes it worse?"

"I'm no expert, Murph. I'm doing my best here." He punched open the locker room door. "But I think it's worth a try. You don't want to shoot like that tomorrow night."

No kidding. But how the hell was he supposed to call her again after the way she'd shut him down last night, saying they'd made a mistake? He couldn't exactly fill out the damn dating survey. That would make it look like he wanted to date anyone but her. She wouldn't even buy it.

As they entered the locker room, all eyes turned his way. At first, he figured the guys were gauging his mood after the missed shot attempt. But then Alexandre, the backup goalie, stepped forward.

"Murph, you know the ladies, they wait for you."

The kid's Russian accent was thick and his syntax a little sketchy, but Kyle could usually figure out what he meant.

Now he wasn't so sure. Twenty teammates wouldn't be standing around gawking over a couple of women waiting for a player.

"What ladies?" He looked around, hoping someone else would clue him in with more details.

Leave it to his smirky position rival, Archambault, to clarify.

"Professional matchmakers." Leandre was already finished with his shower and reeking of cheap cologne in his street clothes. "Apparently Marissa was just the first in a long line. I went out to the lobby a minute ago and you have your own private fan club of matchmakers waiting. One of them has a video camera. I thought she was a reporter."

The last freaking thing he needed before a game when his play was already off.

"You can walk out behind me," Axel joked, flexing enough muscle to provide a human shield for anyone on the team.

Kyle wasn't sure how he'd get out of the arena without speaking to them. But he was damn sure where he'd go when he left the rink. Marissa Collins had somehow gotten him into this mess. So she, in all her infinite matchmaking wisdom, would tell him how to get out of it.

After that, he was going to kiss her until the team flight left for Pittsburgh. With any luck, a thorough taste of Marissa would take the edge off. Because this time, he wouldn't be the one to pull away.

MARISSA JUMPED WHEN the doorbell rang downstairs.

Her mother was finally sleeping peacefully after a difficult physical therapy session that morning. Brandy had been frustrated and tearful with her lack of mobility, finally demanding the physical therapist leave. The encounter had been exhausting for all of them, ending with a call from the rehab center suggesting they move Brandy from the house into full-time rehabilitative care.

A step Marissa had been fighting tooth and nail for weeks.

"Please don't ring again," she muttered to herself, flying down the stairs to the main entrance, which no one used but strangers.

Probably neighbors selling Girl Scout cookies or something. And how could she tell those cute faces she was flat broke?

Wrenching open the door before she'd thought of a good excuse, she was surprised to find Kyle Murphy there, his finger hovering over the doorbell.

"Wow. You're a far cry from a Girl Scout, that's for sure." She drank in the sight of him by daylight.

Green eyes, dark hair, sculpted cheekbones and square chin. A nose that took a wrong turn midway and somehow only made him more gorgeous, possibly because it broadcast a "don't mess with me" vibe. Hard to believe she'd kissed a man that looked like him.

"I take it you were expecting someone else?" He shoved his hands in the pockets of a dark blazer that he wore over a white T-shirt with jeans. "I'm afraid I'm not selling any cookies."

His voice did pleasant things to her insides, the sound humming over her skin and tickling up the back of her neck. What was it about him that appealed to her at a gut level? Because she'd seen plenty of good-looking guys in the years she'd toured with her mom—pop stars, actors, Hollywood royalty—and none of them had ever turned her insides out the way Kyle did.

"No one usually comes to the front door except for people trying to sell me something." She wondered if she really needed to invite him in. A sixth sense told her if he crossed the threshold, he wouldn't be leaving anytime soon.

Her heart rate had revved into high gear the moment she'd spotted him at the door. Now it sent the blood inside her body into a dizzying high-speed cycle. Apparently, she'd forced herself to be objective about men and dating for too long. Some wild and decadent impulse inside her was rebelling now...practically pounding to get out and have its way with the man standing in front of her.

"You should empathize. You're a fairly hard-core salesperson yourself." He drew out the matchmaking questionnaire she'd given him the night before. She recognized the creamy color of the stationery.

But she wasn't sure she recognized the tone behind his words. Was he upset with her because of last night? Because she'd told him it was a mistake for them to be together?

"I won't be pitching my services to you anymore." The finality of the statement unsettled her. She couldn't imagine not seeing him again. "I shouldn't have come on so strong."

Hearing how that sounded, she rushed to clarify.

"I mean, I shouldn't have pitched my services so

forcefully." She didn't want it to sound as if she'd thrown herself at him in a personal way. Although, there was no denying she'd all but melted in his arms.

"I agree. But lucky for you, I've thought of a way you can make it up to me." He leaned forward to peer inside the house. "Can I come in or am I going to have to proposition you in front of the whole neighborhood?"

"Proposition?" Foreboding mingled with anticipation as she debated the wisdom of having him in her mom's house. Marissa had moved into a converted guest cottage after the accident so she could be close to her mother all the time. Technically they lived in separate buildings, but they were within shouting distance if any of the caregivers had problems. No doubt that was how Kyle had found her, since her business card contained the address for the smaller building in back. "I don't know. I'm not alone."

She sneaked a peek toward the dining room but didn't hear anything from her mother.

"We don't need to be alone for this." His smile was pure bad boy. "Although I'm glad to know you're thinking along those lines."

His words smoked over her with phantom heat.

Her mouth dried up and she couldn't think of a comeback. She couldn't have denied it if she tried.

"I'm here because I need your help," he said finally. "I just want you to tell me how to get a rabid pack of professional matchmakers off my case."

And didn't that deflate her ego? She should have known he wouldn't be chasing after her in the cold light of day for romantic reasons. Speaking of cold, the chill of a northern spring reminded her she'd let far too much cool air in the house. But then, Kyle had a knack for sapping away all her normal good sense.

"All right." Stepping back, she gestured him inside. "Just give me a minute to settle my mother with her afternoon nurse and we can go talk in the guest house."

Why worry about being alone with him when he was only here to elude the rest of the matchmaking world? Obviously, she'd succeeded in pushing him away the night before. So how come she didn't feel relieved?

"Seriously?" He stepped into the foyer and she shoved the door closed behind him. "I didn't think it would be that easy convincing you to help."

"Maybe I feel bad about the hard sell last night." She waved him deeper into the house, away from the dining room and toward the addition in the back where an airy family room looked out over the pool. "Come with me."

"This is an impressive house." Kyle peered around the family room, where overstuffed chairs mingled with antique Mexican furnishings. Amps and sound equipment collected dust on one end of the space where framed album covers and news clippings covered one wall. "You didn't mention your mother is Brandy Collins."

She tensed, never prepared to talk about her mom's accident. Months later, it was still too painful, mostly because she didn't know what the future held for recovery.

"I moved out of an apartment downtown last fall after her accident." Everyone knew about the car crash, which had occurred after the kick-off concert of Brandy's first tour in two years. The story had made national headlines, and was still a feature in the entertainment news long after the regular media had finished talking about the accident. "It's easier for me to be here since she has a lot of appointments and needs extra help. I live in the guest cottage out back."

"That's really good of you." Taking her hand, he folded it in his. "It must be hard for you to take on so much."

Most people asked a lot of questions about her mother. Expressed their love of her music and their prayers for her recovery. All of which Marissa was always grateful for. But just now, having Kyle take a moment to acknowledge her sacrifice and her role in the ordeal warmed her heart.

More than that, it made her realize one of the reasons she was so attracted to him. He might be wealthy and famous, a superstar in his own right. Yet he was incredibly real. A genuinely down-to-earth, relatable guy. And having known plenty of famous people, Marissa realized how rare it was to maintain that kind of grounded attitude in the world he moved in. Hadn't Stacy mentioned that Kyle wanted to start a youth hockey camp? Obviously, he was about more than just winning.

"She's my mom," she said simply. "I'm glad that my being here helps her be able to stay at home. She gets confused easily, and I think the familiar surroundings are comforting."

He squeezed her hand hard before letting her go.

"Not every daughter would be so dedicated."

Her eyes burned at his unexpected kindness. She'd been so emotional around him last night and today. It had to be a reaction to all the stress trying to pay the bills.

"Thank you." Backing up a step, she figured the sooner she helped him plot a way to elude the east coast's top matchmakers, the sooner she'd return to her own work. The sooner she'd quit thinking about how much she wanted another kiss. "I'll just be a minute if you want to have a seat. I'll let the nurse know she needs to sit with Mom and then we can figure out what to do about your new fans."

With a clipped nod, he agreed, giving her time to get things settled at the main house. When she returned to the family room, Kyle was reading some of the framed articles about her mother.

"I'm ready." She headed toward the French doors leading out to the pool. "We can talk in the guest cottage so we don't have to worry about waking Mom. It's not extravagant, but it's comfortable."

"After you." Reaching over her head, he palmed the surface of the door, holding it for her.

She slipped past him, catching a scent of soap and aftershave, which did curious things to her insides. Being alone with him would present a challenge, but she couldn't just leave him to the professional matchmakers to tear apart.

After all, she'd started the hunt for him thanks to Stacy Goodwell's insistence. Maybe she felt responsible for allowing Stacy to think she could dictate whom she wanted to meet, something that had bothered her from the start, since it went against her theory of matchmaking. Either way, Marissa hadn't meant to make Kyle a target for other matchmakers in an insane competition dreamed up by Phil Goodwell.

Besides, maybe Marissa didn't like the idea of Kyle

being forced into the dating pool. Why should he have to date Stacy just because her father was a powerful man who might sponsor Kyle's dream of a youth hockey camp?

The idea of him dating other women inspired a possessiveness she had no business feeling.

By the time she reached the guest cottage, her hands were shaky as she slid the key into the lock. Because of her mother. Because of stress.

Even as she tried to make excuses, she knew that wasn't why.

"Let me." Kyle's hand covered hers on the key since she'd apparently forgotten which way it turned.

His powerful body sheltered hers from the breeze, never touching her but making her utterly aware of his presence. She closed her eyes, breathing in his scent. Feeling his warmth. His nearness.

Too soon, he had the door open, his hand falling away from hers. By now she was jittery, the way she'd felt in the days when she drank too much caffeine and didn't eat enough breakfast. Only this time, it was a case of too much sexual frustration and not enough Kyle Murphy.

Half stumbling inside the cottage, she stepped on the ice-blue shag carpet in a living area that was a nod to the seventies and the disco-era. Daylight filtered in the half-closed blinds, but the room was dim with no lights on. Danish modern furniture and an iconic pole lamp with brown metal shades blurred in her mind, a dreamlike backdrop for the only thing that seemed clear in her field of vision.

A strong, attractive athlete who looked at her as if

she was beautiful. He followed her inside and closed the door behind him. The fact that he locked it sent a shiver through her. She swallowed hard.

"I don't know why I thought I could be alone with you." She had no willpower when it came to Kyle. Hadn't she seen as much when he'd kissed her the last time? She'd been ready to climb into his lap and strip them both naked.

"Maybe you realized that last night was special."

Or maybe she was just crazy. All she could think about was the way it had felt to have his hands on her. His lips hot on hers.

"Which, in the end, didn't go so well." She cleared her throat since her voice seemed to have dwindled to nothing.

"Only because you insisted on saying it was all a mistake." He stepped closer, making his intent clear.

Her heart raced. She wanted to say something, but words seemed inadequate to express the tumult of feelings and sensations swirling inside her. He'd been so kind about her mom. So thoughtful about backing off when she'd panicked after their kiss.

"I don't think it was a mistake," he reiterated.

Her heart beat so loud now she could hear it in her ears.

"The only error we made was stopping too soon." His hands slid around her waist and she was lost.

No, she'd been lost from the moment she'd brought him here—to the privacy of the guest cottage—where she could have him all to herself.

"How did you sleep last night, Marissa?" he asked,

breathing the question so softly over her ear that her skin tingled all the way up her spine.

"Not so well," she answered honestly, arching her neck in the sincere hope he would kiss her there again. "I contacted my client. Told her I'm withdrawing from the race to secure you as a date for her."

His lips molded to the column of her throat, tasting her in slow sweeps of his tongue.

"Thank you." He breathed the words against her neck, a warm and minty tickle of air that gave her goose bumps.

Sensation tripped down her shoulder and circled her breast, making her back arch with the need for more contact.

It might be crazy, but Kyle was the only good thing to happen to her in months. And he was better than good. He rated off-the-charts delectable. This time, there would be no stopping.

7

K YLE LIFTED HER OFF her feet. Crushed her to him. Kissed her until he couldn't breathe.

He backed her out of the living area, seeking somewhere to lay her down. Moving blindly, he felt his way down the hallway, protecting her body and not caring what he ran into with his own. Her fingers combed wildly through his hair as she kissed him, her tongue stroking an erotic rhythm over his.

Her orchid scent heightened as her body heated up. She tugged on his jacket sleeve with an impatient hand and he realized she wanted him to go left.

There must be a bedroom in that direction.

Grateful, he edged inside the dim room where the curtains had been fully drawn. A dark shape tucked into a corner looked like the bed. Before he could bring her there, she shifted downward, freeing herself from his arms.

His caveman brain—calibrated solely for sex— couldn't process what was happening. Stopping didn't compute. But then she began unbuttoning her blouse, her pale fingers flying over the fastenings.

This, he understood. Shoving off his jacket, he yanked his T-shirt up and over his head.

"Wait," she pleaded, a soft palm on his bare chest. "I want to see you."

For a moment, she disappeared and he was tempted to follow despite her dictate. But she returned from somewhere—a bathroom off to one side, he thought—with a fat candle burning on a silver tray. The warm light played over her pretty features, casting her skin in a golden glow.

Leaning forward to place the candle on a night-stand, she gave him a gorgeous view of creamy breasts swelling above a pink lace bra. Her half-opened blouse framed the display, making his mouth water for a taste.

"Good idea," he managed to say, his voice throaty and hoarse with hunger for her. But he wanted to show her he hadn't gone totally sex-crazy. He could still appreciate the finer points of taking their time.

Even if blood flow to his erection robbed his brain of vital oxygen.

"I'm out of practice," she whispered, hovering awkwardly over the candle with her glasses steaming up.

"I'm glad." He hadn't meant to say it quite so fiercely, but it was the truth.

He admired her sweetness and her honor, liked the fact that she was careful with herself. So if she needed a little extra time, by God, he was going to give it to her.

"I don't know what you're expecting, but I'm not very…" She seemed to cast around for words, her sexual hesitance making his throat dry up.

How had he gotten so lucky to be with her?

"I only have one expectation," he explained, crossing the bedroom floor to retrieve her since she showed no signs of coming back to him. "I expect I'm going to die any minute now if I don't touch you more."

It was a pressing imperative to put his hands on her. Mold her against him. Taste her thoroughly.

"Sounds serious," she murmured, sliding her glasses down and setting them on the dresser.

"You have no idea." He stopped inches away and undid the last three buttons on her blouse.

A soft breath hissed between her teeth as he pushed the pink cotton off her shoulders, letting it fall to the carpet.

She was thin and delicately made. The gentle swell of her breasts was perfectly proportioned for the rest of her. Unable to resist another second, he skimmed a hand beneath one pink bra strap and let it fall off her shoulder. The cup rolled forward, stopping just before it revealed anything.

Leaning in, he kissed her there, on the top of that plump rise. He licked her and she shivered, a raw moan bubbling up from her throat while he sought the tight crest of her nipple. Finding it, he suckled hard, drawing her deep in his mouth to make her forget about anything but him. This.

He kept her there, working the tight nub with his tongue so his fingers were free to explore. With one hand, he undid the clasp on her skirt. With the other, he tunneled into her hair beneath the loose knot at the back of her head. This time, he knew where to search for the pins, freeing them to unleash the spill of dark hair.

Releasing her for a moment, he edged back to admire his work. The tousled hair and flushed cheeks. The swollen mouth and taut nipple that peeked over the top of her bra cup. While he watched, her skirt began to slip, and he helped it down her narrow hips. Her lace-and-ribbon pink panties were pretty trappings beneath her conservative clothes.

"So?" She toyed with the bra strap that hadn't fallen off her shoulder yet. "I've satisfied your curiosity about what I look like undressed. I think you owe me the same courtesy."

"As much as I'm loving the view, I wouldn't call this undressed." He traced the top hem of her panties, hardly daring to believe he was going to have her. "There's a whole lot more I want to see."

"I expect payment in kind." She tilted her head in a flirty look and reached for his belt buckle, her fingertips brushing his abs and making him fantasize about her hand wrapped around him. "Shall I do the honors?"

He throbbed in response—a definite affirmative. But he didn't trust himself. He needed to maintain control if he wanted any shot of making this right for her.

"I can go faster," he argued, taking over the task. In a blink, his pants and boxers were on the floor and he had the distinct pleasure of watching her eyes widen.

She smiled appreciatively.

"Very nice." Palming his abs just above the tip of his erection, she leaned close to whisper in his ear. "But I might need a little help getting ready for all that."

He strained to be inside her. To stroke himself against the tender softness of her thighs. Higher.

Ruthlessly reining himself in, he lifted her off her feet and dropped her gently in the center of the bed.

"My pleasure," he said roughly, hanging by a thread. He was wound so tight it wouldn't take much to set him off.

For a moment, he simply let his gaze wander over her. She looked so good everywhere, he didn't know where to begin. Then, directing his attention to the places where her lingerie still covered her, he started with the front clasp of the pink bra.

Freeing her breasts, he lavished them with kisses, nips, teasing licks. When her back arched for more, he kissed his way down her body, lingering in the narrow depression of her navel. He listened to her breathing grow deeper. Then faster. Then turn to frustrated gasps as she hooked a thumb in her panties and inched them lower.

A beautiful sign she wanted more.

Gently, Kyle caught a bit of the lace in his teeth and dragged the fabric lower. Lower. The candlelight danced warm shadows against her skin as she rocked her hips closer. When he had her naked, he pressed kisses along her inner thigh. Her sweetly urgent sighs drove him on, a reward for his patience. His restraint.

Her legs shifted against him as he reached the apex of her thighs. Her fingers twined in his hair and the orchid scent of her skin made him desperate for a taste of her.

His restraint slipped and he covered her sex with his mouth. He'd meant to tease and tempt her, to build the heat between them. But the need to have her was riding him hard now. The slick sweetness of her almost sent him over the edge. Just knowing she was this hot, this ready, was killing him.

Gripping her thighs, he made more room for himself. She trembled against his tongue, her whole body quivering. He traced the hot core of her, circling round and round while her short nails scratched into the bedspread on either side of her. He tried to spin out the pleasure, staving off her finish while building the heat. But soon, he couldn't hold back.

Pressing a kiss to her sex, he left her. He wanted to bury himself deep between her legs, but he couldn't recall getting out a condom and his pants were on the other side of the room. She solved the dilemma by tearing open a foil packet she'd retrieved from somewhere. Bless her.

He closed his eyes when she rolled the condom on him, her soft hand as lethal as a tongue stroke. Capturing her wrist, he pulled her back. Then, with a thrust of his hips, he sought the place he'd wanted to be ever since he laid eyes on Marissa.

Inside her.

MARISSA HAD BRACED HERSELF for the feel of him, but her imaginings paled in comparison to the reality of Kyle. She'd never had sex like this. She'd been with men who moved on the fringes of life—like her. Kyle lived it. Embraced it. Grabbed it with both hands and ran.

And oh, she could feel that in the way he touched and kissed her.

"Are you okay?" He held himself very still after the first easy thrust of his hips.

She knew he was holding back. There was more for

her. He'd waited because of her. Because she'd told him she might not be ready for all he had to offer.

But she was *so* ready now.

Arching her hips, she took all of him. It wasn't graceful or smooth, but it felt so damn good she wasn't even the slightest bit sorry she'd taken the initiative. She could tell from his expression—eyes closed, the cords in his neck straining—that he liked the way it felt.

She wrapped her arms around him, savoring every second of having him so close. He was a beautiful, well-made man, his body eye-poppingly masculine. And she had him all to herself. Her body hovered near to fulfillment, her sex humming with frantic nerve endings just waiting for their moment to sing. Yet she didn't want it to end. She wanted to roll around this bed with Kyle wrapped up in her arms for hours. Days.

Lightly, she bit his shoulder then kissed it. Bit and kiss. Licked the salty path of his skin sheened with a hint of sweat from holding back.

At least, she'd like to think that's what it was from. Even now, he started an easy rhythm with his hips. Staved off the inevitable completion with a slow stroke in. Out.

His gaze locked on hers in the candlelight and her heart did a flip inside her chest. Men like him had never noticed her. She had no idea why he seemed to. But there was no denying the attraction. They didn't need to put words to it since it was simply there. All the time.

"I want you all day," he told her, the sentiment echoing her thoughts. "I hope you can clear your calendar."

"I'm not sure," she admitted. "Better make now perfect just in case."

"Don't say that." His thrusts grew harder. Deeper. Faster.

"I'm serious." She knotted her fingers in the bedspread, anchoring herself against the temptation to become swept away by him.

"I know." He dipped down to her breast and circled the tip with his tongue in a way that reminded her of other things he'd done to her. Sweet, wicked things that made her breathe faster now. "But if I was going to make it perfect this time," he continued, pinning her hips with his and moving them in a slow circle that took her breath away. "I would have made you come first with my mouth."

Just hearing the words undid her. She flew apart with a cry, her legs shaking and her body rocking with hard spasms. The power of it rushed her in waves and she had no choice but to let it take her.

He followed her before her release stopped so that their shouts mingled at one point, each at the mercy of something lush and wild.

She rolled to her side on the bed, her body still subject to aftershocks as he held her. It was the most transcendent sex she'd ever had, and she clung to Kyle's shoulders to steady herself in the long, silent moments afterward. Her mind cleared slowly as rational thought returned.

The most rash and reckless thing she'd ever done could come back and bite her. She could lose her credibility in the matchmaking business. Fail her mother completely. But she hadn't been thinking and she'd been caught in an attraction unlike anything she'd ever experienced.

She'd been blinded by attraction once before and it hadn't turned out well. And what she felt for that guy paled in comparison to the industrial-strength magnetism of the draw between her and Kyle.

Now she just had to hope that her sanity returned. That she could maintain perspective on this wild hunger she felt. Maybe if she compartmentalized it—allowed it to be just physical, just temporary—she could retain a shred of objectivity where he was concerned. Because no matter how much the consequences taunted her, she already wanted him again.

8

STACY WAS GOING TO LOSE her mind if Marissa didn't answer her phone soon. She'd started calling her early in the afternoon but hadn't left a message. Once she started talking about her encounter with Isaac, she was afraid she wouldn't stop. And the two-minute window to leave her message on voice mail wouldn't be nearly enough.

What could Marissa possibly be doing that would keep her away from her business line for so long?

Now, ten calls and two hours later, Stacy prowled restlessly around her house as she cradled the phone against her ear. Her ankle still hurt from last night, so she hobbled more than prowled, but she hated the idea of sitting still.

She'd sat still in life for too long already.

"Hello?" Marissa's voice came through the line.

"Thank goodness you're there."

"I've been…in a meeting. But I took a break and saw you'd called a few times. What's up?" Her voice sounded soft. And sort of happy, too. Her meeting must be going well.

Unlike Stacy's day.

"My life is a disaster," she began without preamble. But she needed to get this out in the open before she lost her mind. "I've allowed my father to pull the strings for too long and I don't know how to make him stop. I don't really care about meeting Kyle Murphy."

"Wait. What—"

"It was a dumb idea to say I wanted to meet him, but I thought it would buy me time to meet other guys." She'd always tried to work around her dad passively, taking the path of least resistance since her father could be so very formidable.

No more.

"I thought you had a big crush on him," Marissa protested, not understanding Stacy's plan.

"My *dad* was gung-ho about the matchmaking, and I figured a big hockey star like Kyle would never agree to meet me. Ideally, while you tried to make that happen, you would have also found other dates for me. Realistic ones." She sighed, hating that she'd gone about everything so ass-backward. But she really had thought a matchmaker could help her sift through guys who might not be good for her. Meeting Isaac made her realize she didn't want help figuring out her romantic life. "Little did I know my father would think me snagging a hockey player would be a brilliant idea."

Stacy paused in pacing around the living room. She had two Chihuahua mixes following her and both of her little dogs seemed dizzy from running in circles. She scratched the smaller one—Tink—under the chin.

"You have to talk to your father." Marissa didn't sound as happy now. She sounded vaguely irritated, but mostly insistent. "He's got every matchmaker on the east coast vying to set you up with Kyle."

"I will. Soon. But I didn't call about that. I met someone else. Someone I wish wanted to get to know me better…" Her heart squeezed at the thought of Isaac being completely unmoved by her suggestion that they get together. He'd thought she'd made a clever joke. "But meeting him made me realize that I need to get out from under my father's thumb if I'm ever going to connect with guys who see *me* and not my dad's money."

Isaac hadn't known she was an heiress. She got the feeling he wouldn't be impressed by money, anyway. When she'd checked him out online, she'd learned he was a big-deal CEO of a technology company, so he had no need to chase her father's dollars. Besides, Isaac had said he lived in his head. She wondered what it was like in there and what ideas could occupy so much of his time that he didn't notice his eyebrows were overgrown or that he needed a shave. Wouldn't it be nice to be thinking so hard she didn't care how she looked or what other people thought about her?

"I'm overwhelmed," Marissa said after a long moment. "I'm sorry, Stacy. It's taking me a minute to process this. Would you like my help with this new guy you've met?"

"I don't know. No." She didn't want to subject Isaac to the kind of hell that Kyle Murphy would undoubtedly go through trying to escape a bunch of greedy dating gurus. Plus, if there was any hope of seeing Isaac again, she wanted to figure that out on her own.

She had already gathered that he was a bit of a philanthropist from the articles she'd read online. Undoubtedly his trip to the Phantoms' fundraiser had been in the same vein. Maybe she would run into him again at another local charity function. Her style features for the paper certainly warranted her presence at that sort of thing.

"Well, I can do a preliminary screen for you at least, to make sure he's legit. Email me his name and I'll take care of that."

"Thank you. I'll email you what I've found so far, but that's not why I called."

"So how can I help?" Marissa sounded confused and possibly a little exasperated.

Which was just how Stacy felt so much of the time dealing with her father. But no more. She was done trying to figure out how to make him listen without offending him. Done letting him make her think she wouldn't succeed on her own.

Last night she'd seen herself through Isaac Reynolds's eyes and she hadn't liked the view.

"I need a new direction. A total life overhaul." Looking around her glitzy home, financed by her father, her expensive lifestyle that she could do without, Stacy felt a new sense of purpose. "I'm going to be writing some new things. Blogging some pieces that will be very different from what I do for the paper."

Her writing voice was big and offbeat. And since she only felt comfortable exercising it in print, she owed it to herself to start using it.

"That's great, but—"

"I hoped you would read them for me before I put them online." She trusted Marissa. She'd met her years ago at a Brandy Collins concert after Stacy's dad had finagled a VIP pass for the show. Stacy had always admired Brandy's exciting stage presence and energy, but after meeting the mother and daughter in person, it was Marissa who impressed her the most.

From the way she handled the people backstage, it was obvious the younger woman was the quiet calm beneath the noise and chaos. And she'd been touched at how she'd guided her mom through meetings with the fans, never allowing anyone to take too much of her time.

Stacy had realized then that her life lacked a Marissa. A stable sounding board who listened and didn't dictate. While Marissa had a Type A parent with a strong personality, just like Stacy had in her dad, Marissa had found a way to work with her mom instead of being smothered by her. Stacy had never mastered that balance of loving her dad without being under his thumb.

"Wow. I'd be honored, of course, though I'm not sure if I would be the best critic."

"That's okay. Just be honest and tell me if I'm taking too much of a risk. I've made some poor decisions in the past, so I'd like an outside opinion before I do something crazy." She swallowed hard, thinking as long as she could afford dog food and rent, she'd be okay. "It's overdue, I know. But I'm finally claiming my independence."

"Everything okay?" Kyle looked up at Marissa from his spot at her stove where he moved a skillet back and forth across a burner. The scent of frying eggs filled the kitchen.

She'd offered to make him something to eat before the team flight to Pittsburgh, but when she'd taken the call from Stacy, he'd finished the job. But as delicious as his cooking smelled, she'd rather have a taste of him since he looked good enough to eat. He'd pulled on his jeans and they hung low on his hips, revealing a network of muscles her fingers itched to trace. But he deserved a break to refuel. He'd caused her to see stars the second time they'd made love. She'd barely recovered when the phone rang.

Now, she didn't know how to begin to answer his question. How could she tell Kyle that Stacy had made him a hot commodity among the matchmaking community without risking her client confidentiality? Could Kyle unknowingly be sacrificing Phil Goodwell's support for the youth hockey camp Kyle wanted to establish by *not* dating Stacy? The ethics of the situation were getting sticky.

"Just a client going through some personal problems. She wanted my advice on career ideas." That was true at least.

"Is that in the matchmaker's job description?" He sprinkled cheese on top of the omelets he'd made and her mouth watered.

Apparently good sex made her ravenous. And Kyle seemed to be a very competent cook, seeming comfortable in her kitchen. Perhaps she had drawn unfair conclusions about him by seeing him as a "star" like her mom. Marissa was used to managing her mother's career and, to a certain extent, her home life, as well, since Brandy Collins had never done much in the way of taking care of herself or her household. But Kyle obviously didn't expect star treatment. Yet another way he was a down-to-earth guy.

"No. But she's become a friend." She hadn't fully realized it until Stacy placed the call. But it touched her heart that the younger woman looked to her for advice, especially when Marissa hadn't been making the best work-related decisions herself lately. She needed to confess that she was…what? Dating Kyle? She had no idea where they stood, but it seemed that she owed Stacy an explanation. "Maybe giving her some guidance will help me figure out some new ideas for my career, too."

Belatedly, she realized Kyle needed plates and forks. She hurried around the kitchen to gather serving items and brought them to the wooden bistro table.

"Don't tell me I've scared you away from matchmaking." He flipped the omelets in half and slid them onto their plates.

She smiled at their gargantuan size. Ravenous or not, she'd be eating the eggs he gave her for a week.

"No. I got into it because I have a knack for it and I enjoy it." Taking the skillet from him, she put the pan in the sink and gestured for him to have a seat. "But you can't rush love for the sake of generating a paycheck, and I'm at a position in life where I need a supplemental income that's more reliable."

Preferably large.

"Because of your mom?" He waited for her to join him before digging in.

"Yes. Matchmaking would support me just fine. I personally don't need a big place, but I don't want to sell my mother's house when her cognitive rehabilitation therapist says it's helpful for Mom to be in familiar surroundings. I won't sacrifice things that anchor her memories when she has such a hard time remembering anything." She thought about their conversation last night and wished she could have recalled a time when she'd eaten too much cotton candy. Whatever days her mom was recollecting, Marissa would have liked to have been there with her.

"But why does the income have to come from you? Brandy is a huge star. Can't you release a greatest hits or something to generate some funds until she's better?" Kyle frowned in thought. "I could check in with my dad for ideas, if you like. Robert Murphy is the king of making something out of nothing in business. He has a whole team of finance guys who might—"

"That's okay." She wasn't sure how she felt about that, tying herself even more to Kyle when she'd been so certain she could maintain her distance. She hadn't had time to think about what this afternoon meant for their future yet. "But that's very generous of you. Thank you."

She knew a little about his family from the preliminary screening that she always did for her clients. The Murphys were based in Boston, where Kyle's father had made a fortune in real estate and property development after starting with nothing more than a popular clam shack restaurant on Cape Cod. He'd ridden the business boom of the eighties, starting a small inn next to his restaurant. Now, he had a global resort chain with his oldest son poised to take over as CEO. Kyle, the youngest biological son, had distinguished himself as an athlete while the other brothers had either struck out on their own in business or turned to the military, each one as competitive as the next, by all accounts.

Kyle shrugged. "It's an open invitation. But what about the greatest hits thing? Is that an option?"

"I know my mom's fans would support something like that, but with so much music available digitally, the profits aren't in releasing a record. The real money comes from touring." She'd already investigated that avenue, and the music industry was much different now than ten or fifteen years ago when a greatest hits album would have generated cash. These days, all the music already existed on iPods and computers. Putting it in a new format didn't lead to big sales.

Taking a bite of omelet, she savored the food she hadn't had to cook. It was an unusual treat for her since she'd done all the food prep for both her and her mother for months. "This is delicious, by the way. Thank you so much."

"Stick with me, kid. I make a mean spaghetti, too." He grinned at her over his fork piled high with eggs.

Did he realize what he was saying? No doubt he'd only meant it as an offhand comment. But what would it be like to see him again? And again?

"Uh-oh." He put his fork down.

"What?"

"I ruined the moment by talking about a future, didn't I?"

"Not at all." Embarrassed for taking the idea seriously in the first place, she wished they'd been able to keep the lighter mood.

"I think I'm supposed to wait a few days before I make another date or something, right?" He shook his head, though he didn't seem terribly serious. "I failed Relationship 101."

"Just as well, since we were both very determined not to have a relationship, right?" She took a big bite, determined to move past the awkwardness. She didn't know where things were headed with Kyle, but she couldn't deny she was extremely attracted to him. So much so, she found it hard to keep away. Plus, being with him had been a welcome break from worries about finances and her mom. She didn't want to ruin it now.

"Maybe." He frowned.

Something in his voice sounded strangely ominous.

"Care to explain?" she prompted, surprised how much she really wanted to know.

"It's been a long held belief of mine that being involved with someone during the play-offs is actually detrimental to my game," he explained, downing the rest of his orange juice. "But this morning, something weird happened at practice."

"Such as?"

"I missed a routine goal. More than one, actually." His eyes darkened to a whole new shade of green she hadn't seen before.

His obvious frustration reminded her how seriously he took his career. She'd gathered as much from their conversation the night before about him not wanting to date. But seeing his mood shift to this level of intensity right before her eyes told her he wouldn't allow anything to get in the way of his sport.

"Do you think it could be from something simple like lack of sleep? I used to help my mother troubleshoot after her performances when she wasn't happy with them, and sometimes it stemmed from rudimentary causes." She'd enjoyed those conversations, even when her mom had been frustrated and upset. Marissa rarely had anything to offer on Brandy's career, but she was good with details. "We'd spend a lot of time listening to recordings or going over video footage for missed cues, and hours later, we'd realize she just hadn't been eating well or something small like that."

"No." He shook his head, quickly dismissing the idea. "I take care of my body the same way the team equipment manager takes care of my skates. I have long-standing, effective routines to maintain optimum performance. I know how long I need to sleep depending if I'm at home or on the road. My diet is dictated by my workouts. The workouts are prescribed by what demands I need to make of my body on the ice. It's very exact."

"That sounds highly regimented," she agreed, intrigued that he treated his body like a machine. "Do you make adjustments as you age? Surely you have different requirements from year to year as you—"

"It's not lack of sleep," he told her flatly. His fork clattered to the plate as he gave her a level look. "I missed the shots because I was thinking about you."

KYLE HAD NOT ONLY MANAGED to fail Relationship 101 while seated at Marissa's kitchen table that morning. He was also failing Romance 101, as well.

He should have known that a woman wouldn't respond well to being told she was the reason behind his flat performance on the ice. Marissa looked offended as she saved her leftover omelet in the fridge and then cleared the table.

"So let me fill in the blanks. You don't normally date women while your team is in the play-offs. But after you went home frustrated last night and played poorly today, you figure you should date me, after all?" She kept her volume even, but the pace of her speech accelerated, clueing him in she was not pleased. "Are you going to head for the rink now that we've slept together to see if your shot is back in top form?"

"That's not what I meant." Although he could see her point. When she summed it up that way, it sure made him sound like a jerk. "I never would have come over here today if I didn't want to see you. Badly. The stuff about my problems on the ice—that's subsidiary to the fact that I really want to be with you."

Rising from his seat, he stepped between her and the table so she couldn't clear anything else off of it without going through him.

Effectively stalled by the barrier of his body, she looked up at him with a touch of wariness in her violet eyes. With her hair down and a fringe of bangs brushing her brows, she appeared younger than when they'd first met. More vulnerable, somehow.

"I don't want to be another prescribed measure to keep you in peak performing condition." Her words were quieter now, her tone perfectly reasonable.

That didn't stop the sting of the suggestion.

"Fair enough," he agreed, dropping his hands on her shoulders. Grateful she didn't seem to mind.

Folding her against him, he held her there, liking the way they fit.

"Where do we go from here?" she asked, the scent of her fragrance still faint in her hair if he breathed in deeply enough.

The hint of perfume had him responding instantly, his body ready for her.

"Mmm." She hummed against him, her hips shifting against him as she noticed the reaction. "I don't know if we can solve our problems that way, but I'll admit it's tempting."

"You're not kidding." Tipping her face up to his, he kissed her. "But if I get sidetracked, I'm going to miss the team flight to Pittsburgh for sure."

"I thought you had today off?" She edged back to meet his gaze.

"I do. It's a travel day, though. We play Pittsburgh tomorrow night. Then there's another travel day. Then we play Tampa Bay. I'll be back in town late Tuesday night. Actually, early Wednesday morning. We'll fly back right after the game."

"Maybe I can see you after your practice Wednesday morning."

He liked that she wanted to see him that soon. But he wanted to see her sooner.

"How about you come to one of the road games?" Today was Saturday. He didn't think he could wait until Wednesday to have her again. Not when he wanted her this badly an hour after they'd gotten out of bed.

"Honestly? I would enjoy the time away. But I really need to focus on my mom." She seemed to hesitate, as if she had more to say.

"If it's a matter of keeping on the nurse for extra hours, I'd be happy to—"

"It's not just that, but thank you. I really need to find an answer to the ongoing financial dilemmas." She worried her lower lip with her teeth. "My mom's financial advisor stole her life savings a few years ago, so her funds are too depleted to be of much help. There's an experimental drug that could help her and I'm determined to afford it. I've got to figure out a way to work harder or leverage some asset I haven't thought of, or…I don't know."

No wonder she'd wanted to match him up with her client so badly. She'd needed to close the deal for a good reason. So much so that he wished now he'd just gone on the date.

"Damn, Marissa. I could have at least had dinner with that client of yours if it meant—"

"Don't." She looked a little bit like the naughty librarian again when she pressed a finger over his lips. "Don't even suggest selling yourself out like that. That was never an option."

Her fierce command—a defense of him, really—made him smile even as he still hated the fact that she was dealing with problems of this magnitude. He needed to find a way to help her without hurting her pride, partly because he felt responsible for putting her in a position where she couldn't provide her client with the introduction that would have been a good payday. And partly because he didn't want to see her so worried and stressed when she was already doing everything she could to take care of her mom.

He'd been raised to put his family first, and although he'd never been in a position where he'd had to make sacrifices for them, he would do it in a minute. He admired that Marissa would do the same thing.

"Okay." Nodding, he plucked her finger from his mouth and kissed the back of her hand. His tongue darted out for a taste. "I just figured that it would be easier to be together on the road since the attention from the matchmakers is going to make private time impossible for a while."

Flipping her hand over, he kissed the palm, too, lingering over the sensitive center.

"Your schedule is public knowledge. Don't be surprised if they follow you." Her voice hit an awkward note as she sucked in a breath.

"You're kidding." He'd lose his mind if he had to face a bunch of stupid media attention because of this. Nothing sucked away personal time and distracted an athlete like manufactured headlines and the questions that came as a result.

"I'm perfectly serious. There are a lot of unscrupulous matchmakers out there and a cash reward is going to attract the worse sorts of practitioners."

"So be my media handler. And my matchmaker handler. Come with me on the road and help me figure out how to steer clear of the distractions." The plan took shape immediately, an ideal solution for them both. "You're good at that kind of thing after managing Brandy's career for so long. You'll have your supplemental income and I'll have my life back to normal."

"I can't sleep with someone I'm working for," she chided him as if it was the most elementary of facts. "Besides, you don't need a handler for the matchmakers. You just need to show the world you're…"

She hesitated.

"In a relationship?" he supplied.

"That would help," she acknowledged quietly, her forehead wrinkled in thought. "But I couldn't possibly go on the road with you now. Maybe you should find someone else."

She couldn't be serious. Not after what had happened between them today. He clamped his hands on her hips and squeezed her closer.

"You owe me a favor for bringing this down on my head, right?" That wasn't totally true because it wasn't her fault her client had requested him in the first place. "And I want you to pay me back by helping me get rid of the matchmakers. I'd like to hire you as a professional consultant."

"I can't take money for spending time with you." she asserted, wriggling away from him. "That's an insane suggestion."

"I'm a celebrity athlete. It comes with the territory."

"Kyle, don't put me in this position." Her practical, I-know-best voice almost shamed him into forgetting about the whole thing.

Until he remembered that one false move during play-off season could cost his team a spot in the championships. With serious injuries a perennial threat, who knew how much of a career he had left to hold the Stanley Cup over his head? Even if he remained healthy, he might not ever play with a team that was a lock for clinching their division—a surefire entry into the play-offs.

"*I* didn't put us in this position. Your client did. Now, I need your help and it's worth a whole hell of a lot to me." He couldn't let her say no. "Consider your mother's experimental drug already purchased. Just, please, don't throw me to the professional matchmaking wolves when I'm this close to achieving the pinnacle of my sport."

For a long moment, she said nothing. And she looked as if she might toss him out on his ear at any moment.

"Besides—" he pressed his case "—I'm trying to develop a youth hockey camp for underprivileged kids. I don't want that announcement to be tainted with interest in my bachelor eligibility and stupid questions about my dating preferences. I want to nip this thing in the bud and make it go away."

Finally, Marissa released a pent-up breath. "The camp is a great idea. Maybe we can be seen together in a public venue and send the matchmakers home before this thing goes any further."

"Thank you." He pulled her to his chest to squeeze her.

The relief that coursed through him was about more than preempting the inevitable media attention with a public date. He realized he was also just glad as hell to know they'd be together again. When had a woman ever affected him like that?

"But I don't think it's fair to accept money for my mother's treatment from you when you're only asking me to state the truth about…being with you."

He noticed the careful way she didn't acknowledge that they were a couple.

"You're doing more than stating it. You're giving up valuable time with your mom to be with me in high visibility places."

"Still—"

"Think of it as a gift if you want." The need to help her went deeper than any attraction. "With the kind of money pro athletes make, we practically have a social obligation to do some good with it. Let me help your mom."

"Thank you." She blinked up at him, her gratitude apparent in her eyes. "I can't thank you enough."

"My pleasure." He kissed her cheek, wishing he'd done more to earn that kind of thanks. She was a sweet, selfless person, taking care of her mom. All he was doing was writing a check. But her dedication made him all the more determined to do more than win a Stanley Cup. He'd contribute something good to society through that hockey camp.

"I'll have to make some arrangements for my mother before I can go. One of her nurses should be able to take an extra shift."

"That's fine. The team flight leaves at seven. I'll see if I can find you a flight that leaves a little later than that." Checking his watch, he realized he'd need to floor it to get home and pack some things before he went to the airport.

She nodded. "Any ideas where we can go tonight to be seen? Or would you like me to do some research on that?"

"I wouldn't have any idea where to begin."

"My mom has had concerts in Pittsburgh before. I'll check my notes to see where we ate or if she went to any media events there."

"Great." He found it hard to walk out the door. "But

I have to admit, I'm looking forward to what comes after our date."

"You think you'll get lucky twice in one day?" She looked skeptical but he could see the hint of a smile lurking.

He leaned in for one more kiss, needing a taste of her.

"I'm a very lucky guy."

9

As a MATCHMAKER, Marissa would have never chosen herself as a candidate match for a superstar athlete.

But maybe she wasn't such a bad choice, after all. She'd chosen to meet Kyle in a popular Pittsburgh nightclub where a local radio station was broadcasting live. As she sat alone at the bar, she admitted to herself that she would never make much of a trophy wife with her average looks and habit of shunning the spotlight. Yet she was skilled at calling in the media, something she'd done often when her mom had wanted to spread the word about an appearance or a new project. It had been simple to round up some well-placed reporters with the promise of a scoop on hockey sensation Kyle Murphy.

Drumming her fingernails on the clear Lucite bar in a club coated with neon signs and pink spotlights, Marissa ordered a ginger ale and waited for Kyle to put in his appearance. She'd only been in Pittsburgh for about an hour. She'd checked into a hotel near where the team was staying and then changed into a more traditional "date night" outfit. As much as she liked her vintage clothes and retro glasses, she didn't want to attract attention to herself with anything too quirky.

Besides, Kyle deserved to be photographed with someone marginally attractive, and Marissa had the costume skills necessary to foster that illusion. Her mother had given her a lifetime's worth of advice about making the most of her dark hair and high cheekbones, as if correctly applied blush could detract from the fact that she had a flat chest and a face that was too square. But tonight wasn't about her.

Kyle had left a blank check for her before he left Philly and she'd simply written it to the drug company for the one-month supply the doctor had recommended. The treatment would begin three days from now, assuming the postal service could hold up its end of the deal.

She'd have to find a way to pay Kyle back at a later date. For now, she could only help him out to the best of her ability.

Where was Kyle?

Paying for her ginger ale, Marissa rose from her seat at the bar to wander the perimeter and look for him. Dance music pulsed through the floor and vibrated her toes, reminding her how long it had been since she'd had a night out. Sure, she'd attended plenty of social functions as part of her matchmaking responsibilities or in helping her mother manage her career. But she regarded those events as work. Now, she walked past a packed dance floor as a guest. Instead of assessing the scantily dressed men and women eyeing for signs of potential chemistry, she would be generating some public chemistry of her own.

With Kyle Murphy.

The idea intrigued her. Maybe it was the way her knee-length skirt skimmed her thighs when she walked, the silk lining teasing her bare legs. Her body still felt sexy and desirable after Kyle's touch back at the guest cottage. She felt as though she still had a visible after-sex glow and she was ready to bask in the warmth.

No amount of cosmetic blush could put color in a woman's face like sensual fulfillment.

"Hey beautiful. Want to dance?" A sweaty, mostly drunk dude wearing cargo shorts and a black silk dress shirt breathed down her neck.

Where was her decoy wedding ring when she needed it?

"No. Thank you." She took another drink of her ginger ale and hoped Kyle would arrive soon. He'd needed to check in with his team and have some kind of group dinner before he met her.

And then suddenly, there he was.

Her very own match. Kyle wore a dark T-shirt under a black jacket. Faded jeans.

His eyes met hers across the bar. Held.

Just looking at him made her heart beat faster. It was a strange sensation winding her way through the crowd of the two-story club while staring at him, feeling his gaze on her. Usually when she trolled places like this, she was purposely conservative, keeping herself out of the mix for professional reasons. But tonight, she felt the electricity of the lights and music, the titillation of a man's hot gaze. Mere hours ago, she'd been beneath him, her fingernails digging into his shoulders as he took her body to never-before-scaled heights.

Sidling through the cloud of perfume and cologne that hung thickest near the bar, Marissa finally reached him.

"Who are you and what have you done with my librarian?" he whispered into her hair, pulling her against his side.

She shivered at his touch, wishing they were all alone.

"I wasn't sure if we might be photographed and eyeglasses can reflect the light." She shrugged. "I thought I'd glam it up a little."

"You look gorgeous either way." His hand palmed her waist. "But too many men notice you like this. I'll have to keep you close."

KYLE MEANT EVERY WORD. He couldn't believe how many guys followed her with their eyes when she wasn't wearing conservative clothes or sporting the twist in her hair. Obviously, some men had no imagination if they hadn't been able to see how hot she was either way. Tonight, her hair fell to her shoulders in a dark, sultry wave. A light silk dress skimmed her slight curves and wrapped at her waist, the skirt swishing against his leg now and then in a teasing caress.

She rolled her eyes. "Everyone looks hot through beer goggles. How about we find my reporter friends and then we can blow this joint?"

"Not a fan of club life?" Thank God. He'd never been much of a party guy. Even in college, he'd been focused on his sport.

"I've seen too many victims of excess in the pop music business to be impressed by the club scene."

She took his hand and stepped toward the VIP room in back. "Come on."

Heads turned as she walked through the haze of purple neon lights as if she owned the place. She might not be Cover Girl pretty, but she had a strength of purpose and a comfort in her own skin that commanded attention. Hell, it seized his like a magnet.

Their path cleared except for a few unwise males who tried to lean into her view to claim her attention. Kyle flexed his muscles like a caveman and moved closer, clamping his hands around her waist on their way to the VIP room.

Every guy in the place needed to know Marissa was going home with him.

Strobe lights flashed, and from the DJ booth, some sort of siren sounded. Like a cue to the crowd, the ringing got everyone screaming.

Ignoring the racket, Marissa spoke to the muscleman guarding the rope at the VIP booth and had the guy lifting the velvet barrier in no time.

"Your reporter friends hang out in the VIP section?" Kyle peered around the smaller room where the music was quieter and champagne buckets sat on every table.

A few of the guys on his old teams would haunt places like this in the summer when their training program wasn't as rigorous. But Kyle always preferred to have his friends over to shoot pool or throw darts. Something a little more competitive than who could toss back more shots.

"I told them to meet us here." She turned around with an apologetic smile. "The tab is on you. I hope that was okay."

"Sure." Didn't matter to him. It was worth far more than a few bottles of Dom to make this matchmaker frenzy go away.

His brothers would give him hell when they found out. Bad enough Ax already knew. Danny—the second youngest and the one who'd broken Kyle's nose once upon a time—would love giving him a hard time about that.

"Hello, Shawna," she said, greeting a young woman at a table full of females in the center of the room.

For the next twenty minutes, Kyle basically watched Marissa do her thing—convincing two reporters for the social pages that she and Kyle were an item—while the reporters' noisy friends drank the champagne he'd provided and took pictures of them. It seemed obvious to him that the members of the media she'd chosen didn't have a huge amount of journalistic integrity to be wooed by a night out and expensive bubbly, but who was he to complain?

She was getting the job done in short order and impressing him even more. No wonder she'd been her mother's manager. She was efficient and charming, but utterly professional. He only had to nod at the appropriate moments while Marissa spoon-fed her contacts some stock quotes about Kyle's goals for the hockey season as an aside to their new romance.

"Anything else?" she asked him suddenly, making him remember he wasn't just here to watch her work. Or to count down the minutes until they'd be alone together.

He straightened, already thinking about kissing her senseless in the limo he had waiting outside.

"Not that I can think of. I still owe you a date to-night." He figured it was okay to flirt with her since they were trying to sell the relationship that he'd always told himself he'd never have during the play-offs.

While the women oohed and aahed about how ro-mantic he was, Marissa turned to him and lowered her voice.

"Did you want to talk about your youth hockey camp with her?" she prompted, like a born promoter. "You might generate some more sponsorships if it's men-tioned in the paper."

"I've already got some interest." Kyle had spoken to the owner of the Phantoms' hockey arena about using the space already. "Phil Goodwell is donating the ice time and some funding."

Marissa frowned.

"But if that falls through, don't you think it would be wise to make sure you have some backups?"

Before he'd made up his mind, Marissa was already relating his plan to Shawna, who took notes on a cocktail napkin now that her PDA battery had died.

Kyle didn't interrupt, letting her call the shots with the media since she seemed comfortable with the role. Still, he was surprised about her strong support of the hockey camp. He'd only mentioned it briefly to her.

"Thank you." He spoke into her ear as they rose to leave the meeting.

"No problem." She peered back over her shoulder, having no idea how much she'd helped him.

"I mean it." He tugged gently on her arm, wanting to be sure she knew how damn grateful he was. "You were amazing back there."

"I got good at keeping my mom's interviews on schedule. Otherwise, she'd chat everyone's ear off."

Not until that moment did he realize how much she deflected attention from herself. He'd seen it in the way she dressed before, but now he understood it went deeper than that. She didn't even take credit for work that she was very, very good at.

"It was more than that." His chest warmed at how easily she'd solved a whole world of problems for him. "I never would have thought of mentioning the hockey camp. I really want to make that happen this year."

He couldn't read the expression that crossed her face, but it vanished a moment later.

"I hope that it helps." She edged closer, her skirt teasing along his leg again in a silken *swish.* "But right now, Kyle, you owe me a date and I intend to collect."

"I CAN'T FOLLOW THIS woman anymore."

Isaac Reynolds frowned at the frustrated voice coming through his phone in his home office. He'd called his head of security for an update on Stacy Goodwell, not a resignation.

"Can't or won't?" Isaac switched open the Skype window on his computer so he could see the guy he'd tasked to keep tabs on Stacy for the next forty-eight hours.

Although preliminary checks into her background suggested she was a privileged local girl who wrote a column for a Philly paper, Isaac wasn't taking chances. His high-tech business full of corporate espionage taught him to trust no one.

"Can't," the head of his security team answered

flatly, turning his phone's camera so Isaac could see his face. Bob Wyatt had twenty years of experience and normally appeared well-groomed and competent. Right now, he looked sweaty, disheveled and pissed off. "Take a look at where we are."

He swung the camera for a jerky view of his whereabouts. Passengers stared straight ahead, packed in tight while the steady hum of a motor made white noise in the background.

"On a bus? To where?" Isaac clicked the window to enlarge the picture. "And where the hell is *she?*"

He hadn't seen her in the pan of the swaying motor coach.

"We're headed to Pittsburgh and she's in the back," he hissed into the phone, drawing attention from the guy next to him, who made a face in the frame beside him. "I can't very well videotape her for you since she's taping the whole damn ride herself."

"That makes no sense." Isaac didn't want to be intrigued. At least not until he was one hundred percent sure she wasn't out to sell his secrets. "Why would she film a bus trip?"

Let alone take a bus to Pittsburgh in the first place. It would be one thing if she was making contact with a buyer interested in having her spy on him. In that case, maybe a bus would have been discreet. But anyone who traded in expensive secrets did so anonymously, not on film.

"She made an announcement to the other passengers that she's filming this for a new video blog." Wyatt rolled his eyes, clearly unimpressed with digital media. With his tie askew and one jacket lapel flipped over to show the felt lining beneath, he seethed into the camera while the knucklehead next to him kept leaning into the shot. "She passed around waivers for us to sign, so I had to come up with an excuse."

"Why didn't you sign, man?" the joker in the seat next to Bob asked him, as if he'd been part of the conversation. "The blog sounds cool. I'll bet it gets a million hits."

"What kind of blog?" Isaac had thought about the mystery woman all day. First, he'd had to research her. But also because she'd said they made the perfect couple.

A sex goddess swathed in silver had asked him out but he'd been too busy worrying she was a spy to notice, let alone say yes.

Dumb. Ass.

"It's called *Diva No More*." This from the helpful Joe in the seat next to his so-called head of security. The guy leaned all the way into the camera frame so that his face was superimposed sideways on top of Bob's. "She's leaving behind the hoity-toity life to become a regular girl."

A scuffle ensued around the camera as Bob told the guy to mind his own business. For a few minutes, Isaac couldn't see anything and he suspected Bob had changed seats.

Diva No More? Isaac remembered their conversation about Stacy's father trying to buy her a man. Her insistence that she needed to make her own mistakes. Could she have gone a step further today? Cut the ties to the domineering dad?

Her life didn't sound like a cover for a corporate spy.

Future video blog queen Stacy Goodwell seemed like a sweet, sexy dream girl he'd been too blind to appreciate last night. Now that he'd researched her background, he wasn't going to let anything stop him from seeing her again.

"Sorry about that—" Bob began.

"I need to know what she's doing in Pittsburgh," Isaac interrupted, wondering how to meet up with her without it being too coincidental. His home office in Philly was three hundred miles away. He could call for a plane and beat her there, but he didn't want to look like a stalker.

"I can tell you it doesn't have anything to do with our competitor." Bob kept his voice low even though he'd changed seats and didn't seem to have an eavesdropper. "She's already announced to the whole bus that she's going to the Phantoms game to write a column on fan style for the newspaper."

The style column was her regular job. Isaac wondered how the video blog would fit in with it, but he agreed with Bob's former seatmate—the blog would be a hit. Stacy's whole dazzling personality was camera-ready. She'd be sought after by ten times the number of guys who probably already wanted her.

And that was assuming the damn matchmakers her father hired didn't try to snag her first.

"Make sure she gets to her hotel safely." He didn't like the idea of thirty-odd strangers on a random bus knowing her whereabouts. "I'll take over for you in a couple of hours. I'm on my way to Pittsburgh."

10

Marissa was in such a hurry to be with Kyle that she bolted out the back door into the alley behind the nightclub.

"Wait up." Kyle practically tripped her in his hurry to get in front of her.

He put his big, muscular body between her and the outside world. She didn't mind that she stumbled into his back. He was fun to hold on to, for one thing. And for another, she thought it was kind of charming that he wanted to protect her.

"It's okay." She grabbed a railing on the landing outside the door where two steps led to street level. "I was just in a hurry to get to the hotel."

"Me, too, but this is still a dangerous neighborhood." He tucked her under his arm, keeping her body glued to his as he hurried her toward the limo. "You can't just prance out into some dark alley alone."

She might have protested the idea that she'd *pranced* anywhere. Except that she heard the worry in his voice. Felt his heartbeat racing under one ear where he held her against him.

Her chest squeezed with unexpected warmth. The driver opened the door for her and Kyle ushered her into a vehicle that could have held at least ten more people.

Kyle exchanged words with the chauffeur that were beyond her hearing. Probably instructing him to take them to the team hotel. Or hers. It didn't matter to her where they went, as long as they excised this raucous heat that had been building inside her since the last time they were together. She just hoped being with Kyle eased the ache for him. The attraction that had started out so physical and out of control was starting to take on a new dimension.

He'd urged her to take this trip with him, insisting she'd be helping him out. But she knew darn well he could have hired a publicist to place an article in the paper a whole lot more inexpensively than what he'd paid toward her mother's medicine. She would repay him one day. But it helped her so much right now. It touched her that he'd given her a way to accept his help without feeling too guilty. Obviously, Kyle had a giving nature, a trait that was apparent in the way he volunteered time to charity, sought ways to help underprivileged kids and even helped her mother. The warmth she was starting to feel for him didn't have anything to do with garden variety lust.

"I told him to take us to my hotel," Kyle explained as he slid into the seat beside her. "I'm on a floor away from the rest of the team."

A smoky blues tune played on invisible speakers while white lights ringed the roof, dimming slightly once the driver closed the door. Shut behind blackout glass, Marissa felt her heart hammering wildly, and her skin tingled with the memory of how he'd made her feel earlier today at the carriage house. She'd been so busy since then—making plans for the trip, arranging care for her mother and contacting reporters—that she hadn't had time to think about what this new shift in their relationship meant. But he'd been so good to her. So considerate and incredibly *thorough* when he'd touched her.

Kyle leaned forward and for a moment, she thought he was going to kiss her. But he reached past her for a remote control on the seat beside her.

"Privacy window," he said aloud before thumbing a button. "Locked." The device clicked into place with an audible hitch. "Doors, locked." Another electronic snap.

He'd sealed them into complete seclusion.

There were no club-hopping voyeurs here. No competition for his attention. But she felt a little embarrassed about the way she'd sprinted out to the street, so eager to be with him. All her barriers were falling away and she wasn't doing a thing to stop them. She tried to steady her breathing.

"A story will make it into the social pages tomorrow, for sure," she informed him, tugging absently at the silk wrap dress that skimmed her knees. "Shawna owes me from a long-ago private interview with my mother."

The stretch limo eased away from the curb, crawling slowly through the dark streets. One blues song faded into another, but the sound Marissa was most aware of was her pulse pounding in her ears. Being alone with Kyle—heading to a hotel—made her light-headed with awareness.

Part of her wanted to act on the sensual rush, while the other part of her feared the emotions winding around the attraction, intertwining with them, making her feel too much.

"Thank you. But right now, I don't want to think about tomorrow." Kyle's voice turned rough with a hunger she understood all too well.

His green eyes roamed over her freely, heightening the awareness she already felt.

"No?" She didn't want to, either. She'd sent a text to Stacy to prepare her for the story that would run linking Kyle to Marissa, but she wasn't sure how her former client would react.

"No. I'm just so damn glad I talked you into being here with me."

His hand rested on the seat between them. Close but not touching. She swallowed hard.

When he lifted his hand, he smoothed a strand of her hair where it rested on one shoulder.

"Did I mention how fantastic you look?" He tugged gently on the strand, extending it toward a shaft of light from one of the overhead "stars" on the limo ceiling.

"I don't usually go all out—"

"You don't need to. You have no idea how attractive you are."

She hitched at the skirt again, oddly self-conscious.

"It's okay. I don't need you to feed my ego. I know my attributes are more…understated. After standing in my mother's shadow all my life, I understand that I didn't win the genetic lottery or anything, but I'm comfortable with who I am."

Kyle was already shaking his head.

"I don't know where you got the idea that you ever stand in anyone's shadow. You command attention, Marissa. You're charismatic. Captivating." He lifted a hand to cup her face and smooth over her jaw. "It's the force of your personality, whether you know it or not. I think you have some of that famous Brandy Collins stage presence. People can't take their eyes off you."

The idea surprised a laugh out of her. "Definitely not. But I think it's nice of you—"

"I'm feeling a long way from nice right now." A growl rumbled in his chest as he pulled her against him, the sound so feral it vibrated right through her. "Believe it. Don't believe it. It's still a fact."

She didn't want to argue with him now, when her blood heated at his touch.

"I'm glad," she murmured, her hands finding his broad shoulders and savoring the feel. "I have to admit I've been looking forward to seeing you ever since my plane touched down."

Her heart pounded with the admission and the memory of the moment. His eyes darkened and he palmed her knee, his hand heavy on her leg. The high leather seats and dark windows created a cocoon of intimacy.

"I wish I could have seen you get dressed." He picked up the remote control again and dimmed the overhead lights until they twinkled like faraway stars. "I would have liked watching you brush out your hair. Slide on the stockings."

He traced the thin line up the back of her calf and she shivered, her skin tightening and tingling. She inched closer, her knees grazing his.

"I don't think we would have made it out of the hotel if we'd been together."

With one finger, he skimmed down the line of the stockings to her heel, then made a curving, slalom run back upward. His progress was slow and steamy, making her picture that same teasing touch in other places. Her bare stomach. Down her hip.

"Do you think we're almost at the hotel?" She slipped her hands under his jacket to touch him through the thin T-shirt beneath. The warmth of his skin made her want to tear off everything between them so she could feel that heat on her flesh.

"No." He edged her skirt dangerously higher, lifting it just enough to expose one clasp holding up a stocking. "How about you let me take the edge off for you before we get there?"

Tugging on the elastic strap, he shifted the lace of her garter belt, a phantom touch along the top of her panties. Pleasure cascaded over her skin, desire pooling in her belly.

The soft tremor of the tires made the seat beneath her vibrate, adding to the fever building inside her.

"Only if I can do the same for you." She wanted to touch him as badly as she wanted to be touched.

Besides, being with him earlier today had only made her more hungry for him, as if she'd churned up some inner sex goddess who demanded fulfillment.

"You don't have to—"

She climbed onto his lap and straddled him, ending that line of discussion. Denim rubbed against her legs, tantalizing her with the warmth of the man beneath.

"I want to." She'd never been the sexually aggressive

kind, but Kyle had been so gentle with her before that she found herself wanting to repay him. Lavish touches all over.

For a moment, he held himself so still she was afraid he wouldn't agree. It was crazy to mess around in the back of a limo. But the doors were locked. And she wanted him so badly....

A bump in the road nudged her forward, her thighs sliding down his and bringing them deliciously close. His gaze dipped south, taking in their perilous proximity.

With a groan, he gripped her hips and drew her down on top of him, his erection branding her sex right through their clothes. Then, a frenzy began as they moved in synch, unfastening hooks and buttons, clips and buckles.

Mindless with need, she stripped away his shirt and unfastened his fly, rocking against him while her fingers worked the buttons. Finding the condoms she'd stuffed in her purse, she laid them on the seat beside him. Ready.

"I don't know what's the matter with me," she whispered to herself as much as to him, confused and overwhelmed by sensations. "I'm burning up inside."

"This will help," he assured her, ripping open the condom and rolling it in place.

She stood up long enough to shed her panties, her legs trembling beneath her until she sat back down on top of him. He still had his pants on, but they'd freed him enough that she could touch him. Position him.

"Let me," he told her hoarsely, clueing her into how much he needed this, too. "Come here."

Fingers sinking into her hips, he edged her lower. Lower.

Her world narrowed to the moment, her breathing mirroring his, her body keenly attuned to every single place he touched her. Her eyes sought his, connecting with him in this crazy, urgent hunger.

For an instant, everything stilled. The car. Her heartbeat. His hands. Suspended in time, she felt something deeper than desire curl through her, an emotion so tender she didn't dare touch it.

Then, as if she'd dreamed it, the world began again. He edged his way inside her, filling her so completely there wasn't any room for thought. Dazed, she could only slide her arms around his neck and hold on tight while he created a rhythm sure to drive them both wild.

She felt the frenzy build again, the raging need that had afflicted her all day. Grateful to lose herself in the heat, Marissa let him lead her, the fire so hot now that the slightest bump in the road would set her off.

Biting her lip, she tried to hold back. Make it last for him. But when their eyes met again, she knew she was lost. Kyle breathed her name so softly she saw it more than she heard it. He relinquished his hold on her hips to skim a touch along the slick folds of her sex. Circling. Teasing. Coaxing.

The orgasm hit her so hard her back arched and her toes curled. A scream of pleasure ripped free from her throat, the release so powerful she collapsed against him, every nerve ending throbbing. Through the haze of lush fulfillment, she felt his release inside her, knew it as his hands fisted at her waist and his body tensed over and over.

She lay slumped against his chest, breathless and dazed. She shifted away enough to recline against him while they recovered.

When the car came to a stop again, she wasn't ready to put her clothes back in place. Kyle had to unwind her limbs and help her rearrange her dress. Her panties disappeared into the pocket of his rumpled jacket.

"Are you ready?" he asked, waiting to unlock the doors with the remote.

With an effort, she shook off the sensual fog and smoothed his T-shirt, the scent of him still clinging to her.

Was she ready? Not even close. She'd just had sex in a limo. Her brain had obviously quit functioning when she met Kyle and she needed to talk to him about it. Did she really want to go back to life on the road with a superstar? To fade into the background and quietly manage behind the scenes, the way she had for so many years with her mom?

For now, though, she just needed to get inside the hotel. Think. Regroup.

Nodding, she lied through her teeth.

"Ready."

STACY GOODWELL HADN'T intended to be an instant celebrity. But as she sat cross-legged at the hotel desk the next morning, staring at the stats for her new video blog, she had to admit, the new star status was kind of fun.

Overnight, her video had gone viral. After she'd uploaded the footage from the bus ride to Pittsburgh, she'd stayed awake in her hotel long enough to watch an amazing thing happen. The hit counter went nuts. A few college kids had stumbled on it and shared it with half their campus.

After that, the *Diva No More* blog had crashed twice and she'd been on the phone half the night with techy types who tried to talk her through reinstating it. But despite the hours that the blog itself had been down, the video had enjoyed more than half a million hits.

All in all, this success felt great as she lounged in her sweats at a cheap bed-and-breakfast that didn't mind pets. Tink and Belle had made the trip with her—traveling under the bus driver's radar last night—and they'd had their own turn in the limelight during the edited video of her adventures called "Leaving Home." She hadn't quite figured out how she could generate an income from the endeavor, but she would. For now, she still had her regular check from the newspaper and she could walk a little taller knowing *she* was calling all the shots—from her bank account to her love life.

A shrill yap from under her chair seemed to remind her she wasn't having much luck with the latter yet. How was it a dog could detect a mood? She picked up Belle and snuggled her close, appreciating the empathy. Isaac Reynolds had laughed at the idea of being with her. Maybe it served her right that she'd gotten a reality check from a guy she liked after how many times she'd given the slip to men who'd hit on her.

She stood up and walked away from the laptop, wondering if she'd find another man who made her feel the way Isaac had. She'd met hundreds of eligible males since she was old enough to date. Not once had she felt so at ease with a guy and attracted at the same time.

Now, peering out the window down to the street level, she debated how to solve her romantic problems—

What was her Caravan doing parked in front of the hotel?

Sure, there were other silver Caravans in the world. She'd tried to bust into one just the other night. But what were the chances one would be parked right outside her bed-and-breakfast? Suspicion growing, she grabbed a navy silk bathrobe covered with hand-painted Hawaiian flowers and marched into the hallway, the dogs *click-clacking* along the hardwood floors behind her.

She just knew that had to be her van down there and that her father was responsible. He must have followed her here. Fired up and ready for a confrontation, if only to point out she was doing fine on her own, Stacy nodded to her hostess while the woman vacuumed a carpet downstairs. Breezing past the registration desk, she levered open the main door and saw a man inside the van.

A very familiar man with thick dark hair and heavy eyebrows that, now that she thought about it, really suited him. A wave of heat rolled through her at the sight of him.

"Isaac?" She stopped in her tracks, realizing too late that she'd failed to put on real shoes. Her orange terry-cloth slippers looked out of place on the pavement.

The man she'd met two nights ago peered back at her through the window, his expression inscrutable. Was he surprised to see her? Or had he known she was here?

With most men, she wouldn't have asked. Then again, with most guys, she wouldn't have cared. But

Marissa had told her that Isaac Reynolds was an internet marketing genius and a techno-whiz who'd made millions before he turned twenty-five. A kid from a poor Detroit suburb who took apart old computers for fun. Something about his quietly sexy charm appealed to Stacy like no other guy. Certainly not Kyle Murphy, who'd only been the decoy romantic interest. She'd been glad to hear that Marissa had made a move on the hockey star, and she'd texted her last night to tell her so.

Tink jumped at the driver's-side door of the Caravan. Stacy lifted her fist to rap on the window when Isaac opened the door, swiveling toward her to step down to the street. His arms flexed as he moved and she remembered what those lean, wiry muscles felt like around her.

"Can we talk inside?" he asked. As if they were going to chat about the weather.

As if he hadn't laughed it up over her foolish idea to ask him out just two days ago. It would be so much easier to be mad at him if he wasn't so hot. What was it about his quiet, thoughtful stares that made her feel like an interesting, alluring woman instead of a replaceable hot babe?

"I don't think so." She folded her arms, silently urging her pets to show a little teeth. Maybe give a warning growl.

Instead, they seemed intent on circling him to death, chasing each other around his heels.

"Okay," he agreed slowly, as if the word had to be dragged out of him. "But do you want to, maybe, put clothes on first?"

For an instant, she was genuinely scared she'd walked out onto the street naked. She wouldn't put it past her to flake out and forget to dress. But no, she wore a perfectly respectable bathrobe over semirespectable pinstripe pajamas. They probably weren't cut out for the commercial area growing up around a few old residential buildings. But she had to think the few folks living on this street must venture out to get their newspapers in a bathrobe now and then.

"No. I'm good, thanks." Although, as soon as she said it, she wondered if the cool spring breeze might inadvertently press the fabric close enough to reveal a little too much.

Instead of arguing with her, Isaac reached back into his van and withdrew a black wool blazer. He handed over the jacket and stood silently.

She blinked back a wave of emotion. Her dad would have launched into conversation the second he saw her and not let up until he'd cataloged all the ways she could have handled the situation differently than storming outside in her pajamas. Isaac just covered her up.

But no matter how much she wanted him, she had to remember, he didn't want *her*. She took a deep breath.

"What are you doing here?" she asked, the scent of his aftershave a pleasant musk in her nose.

"I followed you," he said simply, flooring her.

"Excuse me?" She snapped her fingers ineffectually at the dogs, trying to quiet them so she could hear whatever scant words fell from Isaac's mouth.

"I wanted to know more about you, so I looked you up online. I watched the video and respect what you're doing."

"You wanted to know more about me." She didn't ask why, although the question was burning to come out. But she wasn't going to appear overeager with this guy and...oh, to hell with it. "Why? Why would you want to know more about someone you found lacking just two days ago?"

She snapped her fingers again at the dogs, unwilling to see them cozy up to Isaac. But they just barked at her vague commands, the tiny bells on their collars jingling with the force of their yippy protests. Traitors.

"I didn't find you lacking. I thought you were spying on me." He bent toward the adoring fans at his feet.

While Stacy tried to make sense of what he just said, Isaac scooped up a dog under each arm and juggled them easily until Tink and Belle settled happily against his chest. She imagined what it would feel like to trade places with the canines. To be back in the circle of his arms.

"Why would I spy on you? I didn't even know who you were—" Although, come to think of it, she knew about him now. Some big-deal techno-gadget man. A discreetly wealthy graphics chip maker. "Did you think I was some kind of Gotham City villain out to steal the plans for your microchip? Maybe block out the sun and take over the town while I was at it?"

The sarcasm surprised her since she was usually frustratingly nice to guys even when they didn't deserve it. Yet with Isaac—who still appealed to her more than any other—she said what came to mind. He would probably never understand why that was a good thing. But she'd lived with her nice-girl reflex long enough to appreciate the ease with which she spoke to him.

"It's not a microchip," he informed her. "But I'm flattered you looked me up after the awkward way we parted."

Damn it. Had she given that away? Better not admit she'd also had a professional matchmaker check him out.

"I needed to make sure you weren't a serial killer," she said defensively, unwilling to reveal any more soft feelings for him after putting herself on the line with him last time. She wasn't about to give up her newfound independence.

Some kids rolled past on skateboards, their heads swiveling to take in her outfit. She really should have dressed before storming out here. Her toes curled in her slippers as she sidled closer to Isaac.

"I looked you up, too," he admitted, giving the kids the hairy eyeball until they rolled away. "I know you're not a spy and I'm sorry for misreading the situation."

For a moment, she was wooed by the sound of his voice, so warm and deep. But she couldn't afford to get sucked in by him again. She needed to be more discerning when it came to men. Although he'd sure come a long way to apologize.

"How did you know where to find me?" She didn't remember saying where she'd be staying in her video blog. "Did you honestly drive three hundred miles to find me?"

"Technically? I had my security team keep an eye on you after we met—"

"You followed me?"

"Not me personally—"

"No. Only your *security team*." She grabbed the

lapels of the jacket and squeezed them tighter, peering around the street for spies. "What threat could I possibly have posed to you with my hobbled ankle while I was lost in a freaking parking lot?"

She wasn't offended, per se. Possibly, she was a little flattered to think she looked like a dangerous industrial spy. Before he could answer, she continued.

"I mean, it's one thing to think I was up to no good back at that hotel the other night. But once you found out who I was, Stacy Goodwell the clumsy trust-fund baby—"

"Don't sell yourself short." His words were so sharp it took her a moment to realize he was saying something nice.

"You live in town. You must know how I'm portrayed in the social pages." A double slap in the face since her biggest detractor was a fellow columnist at the paper. "I'm the one who's always tripping and spilling things, talking too loud, making a spectacle of myself on the dance floor."

"You're effusive and passionate." He said it with a straight face.

"Is that my problem?" she asked, scuffing her slipper along a crack in the pavement.

"It's not a problem. It's a beautiful personality trait. And I had you followed because you graduated summa cum laude from U Penn with a business degree. That alerted me you could indeed be working for a competitor. But after more digging, we knew that wasn't the case. I told my team to leave you alone."

Even the degree program had been at her father's

prompting. She'd wanted to pursue something more creative.

"I'm glad you don't think I'm a spy anymore." What might have happened between them the other night if he hadn't been suspicious?

"I think the video blog is great, by the way."

"You do?"

"Yes." He lowered Belle to the street now that the dog had calmed down. How did he know she was the alpha female of the pair? Once Belle was happy, Tink jumped down, too. "It's a compelling concept for a video blog, but better yet, it's a good way for you to show your father you're serious about taking charge."

"I know the break is long overdue, and I feel like a coward for leaving town when the video hit to avoid facing him—"

"That's why you're in Pittsburgh?"

"In theory, I'm here to root for the Phantoms." She stood beside him as they watched the dogs investigate patches of garden around a few row houses. "But I also wanted to put some miles between me and my dad so he didn't end up on my doorstep for hours, explaining why I'd made another misstep."

"In theory, I'm here to watch the hockey game, too." He withdrew two tickets from the pocket of the jacket he'd given her to wear.

The slight touch of his fingertips against her hipbone lingered. A shiver tickled up her spine, and it didn't have anything to do with the cold.

"But you have an ulterior motive?" Her heart beat faster.

"It's threefold." He lowered his voice as an older

couple exited the bed-and-breakfast and strolled past them hand in hand.

"That sounds…well planned." She stayed close to him to ensure she could hear him.

Okay, also so she'd be within easy reach if he decided to touch her. Maybe she could stumble into him again.

"First, I wanted to find you." He ticked off the item on his index finger.

"You've accomplished that."

"Second, I wanted to apologize for thinking you were a spy and missing my chance to be with you." He turned toward her and suddenly she was the center of his intense focus. They breathed the same air, wrapped in the same moment that had turned heated.

"You're forgiven," she blurted, mostly because it was true, but also because she wanted to speed him along toward whatever else he'd come here to say.

The suspense was killing her.

"Three, I'd like to ask you to go out with me tonight. I understand you might wish to ignore the invitation in retribution for the way I misheard yours the other night—"

Stacy didn't let him finish. She was too busy kissing him.

11

KYLE DIDN'T WASTE ANY time after the morning skate at the Pittsburgh facility. He was the first to shower and head back to the hotel; he'd promised Marissa he wouldn't be gone for long when he'd left her early that morning. She'd wanted to talk since the night before, but he'd been concerned that she'd find some new reason why they shouldn't be together, so he'd made a game of distracting her in every way imaginable at his hotel suite.

In the shower. Against the bedroom door. Then, endlessly on the king-size bed. By the time he'd decided they needed sustenance before they touched each other again, Marissa had fallen asleep.

Now, he took the back stairs to his room two at a time, not wanting to deal with any fallout from the pictures taken of him and Marissa in the nightclub. Most of the guys on the team hadn't seen the articles yet, but the coach had gotten wind of it and cornered him about making his love life too high-profile. Nico Cesare had been none too pleased, insisting he hadn't brought Kyle and Axel over from the Boston Bears to make social headlines. He expected good offense.

Kyle regretted that he'd disappointed Coach Cesare since it hadn't been his intention to cause a distraction for his team. But damn it, he couldn't afford the disruption of high-powered matchmakers dogging him for the rest of the season, either, and they'd magically evaporated today. There was no sign of them after practice. No texts on his phone from dating services asking him for meetings.

Marissa had delivered on getting them off his back. Which was perfect, because it cleared the way for him to focus on his game. And on Marissa. He shot like a pro through practice today, a surefire sign that being with her agreed with his game. If he could just get through the end of the season, they could have the summer together while he worked on his youth hockey camp.

It was the most long-term future he'd ever visualized for himself outside of his career goals. Sure, he'd always imagined a wife and kids someday, after he'd reached his potential on the ice.

But had he just really thought of "wife and kids" in the same moment as Marissa? He shook himself, not wanting to overthink something good. Marissa wasn't looking for anything serious and neither was he. She needed to stay in Philadelphia with her mother while he would continue to travel with his team. Who even knew if he'd be with the Phantoms next year? But for now, what he had with Marissa last night had been perfect.

Kyle rapped lightly on the door in case she was still

sleeping, then he used his room key when she didn't answer.

"Marissa?" He rolled his shoulder as he set down his bag, hoping it hadn't been a mistake to forego a session with the massage therapist after practice.

Damn it, he was already messing up his routines to be with her. Maybe when they got back to Philadelphia he'd be able to resurrect the rhythm of his training.

"In here," she called, her voice oddly muffled from somewhere in the bedroom.

The lights were all on in the living area, and he could smell coffee from the pot on the wet bar. On the surface, the room looked like any of hundreds of others he'd stayed in over the years. But this one was different—a whole lot more welcoming—because Marissa was sharing it with him.

"I have time for breakfast if you'd like to go out," he started, winding around a pull-out sofa and heading toward the bedroom. "I don't want you to think I'm a cheap date. Last night couldn't have been much fun at the club—hot damn."

His jaw dropped when he got an eyeful of her still wearing a white terry-cloth towel, fresh from the shower. He wanted her for so many reasons that weren't physical, and yet the power of the chemistry between them was like a hard check to the back. It robbed him of breath and made him see stars.

"Morning." She smiled but pulled the towel tighter.

Part of her natural modesty, or a sign she was already resurrecting barriers?

He bent to kiss her bare shoulder, inhaling the clean scent of her soap.

"I wanted you before I even walked in here," he told her, his hands gravitating toward her waist to smooth over the smooth fabric. "I thought about you all during practice."

He'd practically sprinted to their floor. It boggled the mind to think how much he wanted to be with her after all the ways they'd pleasured each other the night before.

"Did your game still suffer for it today?" She turned in his arms, facing him head-on, the view of the historic district and the Delaware River glittering through a window behind her.

Obviously, she remembered that he hadn't played well the day before when they hadn't even been together yet. He'd sucked then because he'd been frustrated. She'd intimated that was his reason for being with her.

And there was definitely some kind of distance in her voice now. A reserve. He tried to battle back his hunger for her so he could hear her out.

"No," he answered carefully, not wanting her to misinterpret his motives. "I was unstoppable in front of the net. As I should be."

"You certainly don't have a confidence problem, do you?" Her tone was teasing, but she looked at him curiously.

"I've been training for this since I was a peewee player. If I can't make the hard shots, I don't deserve to be here."

"And I thought *I* put a lot of pressure on myself to succeed." Marissa shook her head, her damp hair clinging to one shoulder. "Guess I don't compare."

"It's not pressure," he said, waving away the idea. "Success is a powerful reward."

He backed toward the edge of the hotel bed, taking her with him. He'd been ruthless in distracting her repeatedly last night when she'd wanted to talk, so he would try his best to keep his hands off her long enough to hear her out.

"A reward? Does it really feel like a reward for you when one day of poor shooting has you thinking you don't deserve to be in this league?" She looked up at him as she settled on the bed beside him.

Those violet eyes of hers disarmed him, making him question himself for a moment. But he couldn't start coasting now when he was so close to achieving his goals. Not even for her. But he wouldn't let it come to that.

"The reward comes when I hoist a championship trophy." He'd been visualizing the moment for more than a decade. "Until then, I've got to keep working."

"That's a fierce work ethic," she observed lightly. "I'm glad your practice went well, but I hate to think any wrinkle between us could have repercussions for your career."

A warning note sounded in his ears.

"Wrinkle? Why would there be any wrinkle? Don't tell me you thought last night was another mistake."

She'd said as much about their first real kiss and she'd been dead wrong then, too.

"No." She twisted her fingers through a corner of the bed sheet, weaving the fabric between each digit. "I don't think it was a mistake, but then again, I never seem to have any perspective on my relationships."

Her creamy skin called to him. He wanted to press her to the bed and forget everything else.

"You have perfect perspective. You're with me and that's a great idea." He sensed her pulling away and didn't understand why. The last two nights they shared had been incredible. He was already thinking about how they could be together through the rest of the playoffs. How he could come home to her in his hotel room more often. "Is this about me asking you to help me with the matchmakers? Because we're in the clear now. I didn't see any media vultures or matchmaking types outside the hotel."

"It's not about that." She let go of the sheet and the towel knotted between her breasts shifted with the movement. "I'm grateful for the chance to help you out of a mess I created, and you were more than generous to offer payment for my assistance. I wrote your check out to the drug company to start my mother's treatments, but I plan on paying you back."

"Don't even think about it. The matchmaking debacle wasn't your fault. Although by now, I'm dying to know whose fault it was so I can inform Ms. Entitled that not everything can be bought for a price." He resented the way a high-pressure client had put Marissa in such an awkward position professionally. And it doubly pissed him off that her client had upped the ante by hiring competing matchmakers to try to land him.

"She doesn't feel entitled," Marissa confided. Tucking some of her fallen hair behind her ear, she seemed tense. Nervous? "Hiring competing matchmakers was her wealthy father's idea. I think it was a turning point in an uneasy relationship for her because she's ventured out on her own since then."

"Meaning she's not taking daddy's money to buy her dates anymore?" He found it difficult to be sympathetic when the woman's manhunt had caused both him and Marissa a lot of grief.

"Meaning she moved out of a house her family owned, only taking her clothes and her dogs. I think she really wants to…find herself."

Kyle frowned, trying to interpret her tone of voice.

"You admire her."

She shrugged, the movement shifting the towel and reminding him how much he'd rather be touching her right now. But this was important. *She* was important. And something told him he needed to pay attention to whatever they were circling around. He studied her more intently.

"I'm proud of her. I've known her for a long time and I've known a lot of people *like her* for a long time. Sons and daughters of wealthy, entitled parents. It can be tough to forge your own identity in the shadow of so much success."

"For you, too?" He remembered how professional she'd been at the Phantoms' fundraiser, refusing to flirt with him no matter how hard he'd tried to corner her for a kiss.

She'd been cool, controlled. And, he'd guessed, very sure of herself. Had he read her all wrong?

"Maybe. I took the job as my mother's manager because, quite honestly, she couldn't do it alone. She's a handful for any manager, but she always listened to me. Matchmaking was always the job I loved best, at least until I needed the income and it became more stressful." She toyed with the hem of the towel, her fingers traveling everywhere but on him. "But sometimes I wonder what path I might have chosen if I hadn't fallen into being her manager. In a lot of ways, I was the caretaker even before her accident."

"So you'd like to start over, professionally." He wanted to cover her hand where she played with the hem of the towel, cup her knee and smooth his way up her thigh. But he knew she needed to talk about this. That he needed to listen.

"Someday. When she's better. I've managed someone else's career for too long. It's time to start figuring out my own."

"You should come on the road with me for a while," he offered. "You've been working so hard—"

"And I need to keep working hard if I want to be there for my mother. She has a long road to recovery." Her expression warned him this was a tread-lightly zone.

But damn it, he wasn't just suggesting it for selfish reasons.

"Have you considered other options for her? Getting some more help taking care of your mother?"

She straightened.

"I will not move her into assisted living. She's going to recover. She's so young—"

"I'm not suggesting assisted living. I wouldn't presume to know the right time for a move like that." Although he certainly understood the desire to keep loved ones close. He shared a tight bond with his whole family. "But sometimes we're so close to the people we love it's hard to see—"

"I know." She nodded, her shoulders sagging. "But how can I make changes now when her doctors say that maintaining routine might be helpful for her recovery? This isn't an exact science, and I get a lot of conflicting advice about how to handle her therapy, but I've seen firsthand that she's more relaxed at home than when I have to take her in for appointments. How can I ignore what's best for her to indulge a personal whim?"

"I wouldn't call the decision to go on the road with me a *whim*. I just told the press we were together, so that's got to count for something." Now he was the one with his back up. "Come to Tampa Bay for the next game. See how it feels."

"Just because we tell the press we're a couple doesn't make it so. We both said we didn't want a relationship, right?" She kept her voice gentle. "So if what we have together now *isn't* a relationship, then I think it's just… self-indulgent."

Sex was self-indulgent?

Not until that moment did he fully appreciate that she had very traditional values. Yet the signs had been there from the start. The skirt to the knee and the vintage sixties clothes that had been sexy in a buttoned-up way. Moving into her mother's guest house to care for her when so many people would have let professionals handle her care. Wearing a wedding ring to ensure single men didn't hit on her during her work. Hell, even her job screamed conservative, family-oriented ideals. She worked to bring people together into meaningful relationships.

Happily-freaking-after.

The light bulb that flicked on in his brain over all that was so bright he blinked stupidly, trying to reassess what this meant for them.

"Self-indulgent," he finally repeated. No doubt she'd only made this trip to soothe her guilt over her role in making him a target for matchmakers.

While she was attracted to him, she apparently viewed sex as a hedonistic pleasure until she found the real thing.

Love.

"It would be nice to have the freedom to make the choice to do things just for me." She tipped her forehead to his chest. "I've had more fun with you these last few days than I've had in a long time."

His arms went around her on instinct. And because he really, really wanted to hold her. He'd had a great time being with her, too. Would she feel differently about going on the road with him if they defined the relationship somehow? But this wasn't high school and he couldn't risk complicating things any more.

He'd never intended to make these kinds of decisions while his career was in high gear. He was crazy about her. Might even...yeah. He might have bigger feelings for her, too.

But for right now, he needed to focus on his game. With a win tonight, the Phantoms would clinch their division. A surefire play-off berth.

And not even the hottest woman on earth was going to distract him from achieving everything he'd worked for.

"Stay for tonight's game, okay?" His chest burned

when he thought about letting her go. "But if you still want to leave in the morning, I'll call around and book a flight home for you tomorrow."

ISAAC HAD PLANNED HIS approach with Stacy carefully. He'd drawn up a mental blueprint and considered various executions to increase his chances for success.

Yet he'd never envisioned the level of enthusiasm of her response.

She was in his arms in a flash, her freshly washed hair still damp from a morning shower. With her arms wrapped around his neck, the silk robe and the jacket he'd given her had parted, allowing him to feel her curves through nothing more than thin cotton pajamas.

Her lush breasts pressed against his chest and her mouth fitted to his in a kiss that started out sweet and slowly turned…wow. Too erotic for a street corner. A whistle from the driver of a passing car told him as much even if he'd been too overwhelmed to string the thought together himself.

"We should…wait," he urged, breaking away from the kiss while still holding her close. He couldn't pry himself much farther from her. "This probably isn't the best place for—"

"Making out?" she suggested, her blue eyes full of mischief as she rolled her hips against his.

Without question, she could feel how much he wanted more than a make-out session.

"That, either." He dragged in a deep breath to try to will away his reaction, but Stacy didn't help matters when she smoothed a palm down his chest and dragged her fingers lower.

"Why don't you come inside and warm up first?" she suggested. "You only just arrived."

A gray-haired woman walked by wheeling a small cart with a grocery sack strapped to it, her appearance reminding him to back off the public display of affection. But as Isaac tugged Stacy toward the side of the street, the woman winked at him.

"I don't want to misinterpret this," he began, not trusting his instincts when they were operating on a primal level. "Are you seducing me?"

Her eyebrows lifted. A small smile twitched the corner of her lush lips.

"I'd prefer you seduce me—"

A roar of satisfaction surged through him and it took all his willpower not to pin her to the brick wall of the building and kiss her until they forgot their names. Instead, he spun her in his arms and steered her toward the entrance to the inn. Staying close behind her, he wrapped an arm around her waist to hold the jacket closed over her delectable body.

Ask and you shall receive, Stacy thought to herself, realizing now why she hadn't ever truly voiced her thoughts and her heart to a man before.

She'd been waiting for Isaac. Someone who listened. Someone who looked into her eyes even if he was thinking about her body. And *oh, my,* she could tell he was thinking about her that way now.

His body brushed hers as they walked into the bed-and-breakfast and up the stairs to her room, dogs leading the way. While she opened the door, the hard, muscular strength of him pressed behind her. Something had shifted between them—something besides the obvious—when she had playfully suggested she wanted to be seduced. Judging by the way Isaac marched her into the bedroom and closed the door behind them, leaving Tink and Belle out in the living area by their food and water, Stacy could tell he'd taken her very seriously.

She should have known there was no such thing as a playful suggestion with this intense, quiet man.

"I hope I didn't rush things," she blurted, suddenly self-conscious about her flirtation. "Sometimes I say the first thing that pops into my mind and—"

His dark gaze met hers. He crossed the floor in a heartbeat, lean muscle and long legs eating up the space between them.

"I like the way you think."

She breathed in his words, the notion appealing to her on every level.

"You're going to make me a very happy woman." She knew it on a soul-deep level, trusting her instincts with a gut sureness she'd never felt about anything except her decision to leave home.

Isaac's hands molded to her waist, then slid around to span the small of her back.

"Very happy," he agreed, fingers climbing up her spine in a smooth dance that sent shivers down her spine. "Also, very excited."

Reaching the collar of her pajamas, he slid one hand beneath to caress the bare skin of her shoulder. The warmth of his palm rasped over her flesh with tender care. His touch was thorough. Thoughtful. It stole her breath to think about what it would be like to have all that Isaac intensity focused on her body.

A fire leaped in her belly. Ribbons of pleasure unfurled from the place where he stroked her.

"I've been fantasizing about you," she confessed, splaying her fingers over the soft cotton button-down he wore. Through the fabric, his heart slugged hard.

"I hope you describe those fantasies in painstaking detail for me one day." He eased open the top two buttons on her top. Parted the fabric. "But if this moment gets any better for me right now, I might not survive it."

Cool air hit her breasts, the tips tingling and sensitive. She wanted to rip off the rest of her clothes and his, too, but then again, she didn't want to miss seeing what he did next.

Shrugging off her robe, she wiggled out of her pajama top at the same time. The loose fabric pooled at her feet and she stepped out of it, her toes almost on top of his as they stood chest to chest.

She was so ready for this. For him. Desire simmered beneath her skin, a warm current flowing to every pore of her body. But he didn't crush her to him. Didn't fall with her to the bed. He bracketed her face with his hands, smoothing his thumbs over her cheeks as if he would memorize the shape. Then, spearing his fingers into her hair, he pulled her mouth to his to brush a kiss over her lips.

Liquid fire danced in her veins. He kissed like a god, sure and knowing, claiming her mouth like an erotic explorer, leaving no place untouched. All the while, his hands skimmed her body, arousing erogenous zones she never knew she had. The back of her neck. The side of one shoulder. When he circled the soft indent of her elbow, her knees went weak.

Her whole body burned. Isaac captured her lower lip and tugged it between his teeth, the act so overtly sexual she felt a little preliminary spasm deep between her thighs.

Hungry for more, she fumbled with the buttons on his shirt, wrestling the discs through the stitched cotton. Her progress slowed as she peeked at what she'd unveiled. For a glorified techno-dude, he had the body of an Adonis. Smooth, sculpted muscle. No fat. No overinflated he-man bulk.

"I want to feel you against me." Her fingers were hung up on the cotton, a cocktail ring twisting in a buttonhole. Why hadn't she taken the silly thing off when she'd dressed for bed?

"Let me." He freed her finger and then slid the jewelry off, settling the fat green agate on the nightstand. "You don't need any decorations, Stacy. You're perfect."

In no time, he had his shirt off and his belt was gone. His hands went to his trousers but she stopped him.

"I'll be careful," she promised, palming the length of his fly and feeling the breadth of what lay beneath. "In fact, I could do this with no hands."

She lifted her palms in the air and licked her lips to prove the point.

His mouth covered hers instantly, capturing her tongue and circling it with his own. His hips strained against hers now and she loved the urgent feel of his movements as he dragged her pajama pants down her thighs. She backed toward the bed.

He followed, lips still sealed to hers. And despite her offer to undress him the rest of the way, he shed his pants and tossed his wallet on the mattress, no doubt putting a condom within easy reach.

"Thank you for finding me," she murmured, eyeing his boxers with anticipation. "I'm so glad you came for me."

His grin was wicked. Feral.

"Now it's your turn." He cupped her bottom and guided her down to the bed. "Are you going to come for me?"

He had no idea how much she wanted him. She felt the tremor of her first orgasm swirling already. They'd kissed for so long and she'd fantasized about him since the moment they'd met.

And *oh,* it felt like heaven when he lowered his head to her breasts and drew the tip lightly between his teeth. Rolled the nipple along his tongue. A moan bubbled up her throat, her thighs shifting restlessly beneath him.

When he touched her there, one finger dipping into her sex while he cupped her mound, she flew apart. Sensation rocked her, her release rolling over her while Isaac coaxed more and more from her.

She wanted him inside her, feeling the storm along with her. But her breath dragged in and out of her lungs so hard she could barely speak. By the time he rolled the condom into place, the last orgasm had finally slowed down, leaving her blissfully sated and somehow hungry for him at the same time.

His erection jutted toward her, exactly what she craved and more. She reached for him, wanting to stroke the length of him, but he caught her wrist and stopped her. Instead, he guided himself closer to where she wanted him. He entered her slowly, hands bracketing her shoulders on the bed. The feel of him inside was indescribable completion.

Locking her legs around his waist, she held him there, arching her hips to his to bring him the same pleasure she'd just felt. Only now, the sensation built for her again, too. He sucked in a breath and held it as he held himself back. But the slick friction drove her wild, her fingers seeking purchase on his back as she drew closer and closer to that point of no return.

"Wait." Isaac stilled her with a hand on her shoulder, the heel of his palm resting on the swell of her breast. "I need to touch you."

"I'm close, though," she admitted, knowing one stroke of his finger could send her over the edge again.

"That's okay. So am I." He brushed a kiss over her lips, assuring her he was right there with her.

When he reached between them to touch the taut nub of her sex, she let herself go, her back arching as pleasure dragged her under again. Only this time, Isaac's control broke, his hips sinking all the way into her and pinning her against the bed. His shout put the dogs in a frenzy on the other side of the door, his voice mingling with hers. A chorus of absolute perfection.

His smile mirrored hers when she was able to move again. Locked together, she could have sworn they shared the same emotion. The same thoughts.

"This is going to be the best first date of my life." He rolled her to her side so they could lie together.

"I'm really looking forward to it, too. But before that, I want to know everything about you. Your job. Your family. Why a smart guy like you would ever fall for a girl like me.... I want to know it all."

It was a new beginning. She didn't know enough about him, but she looked forward to learning everything.

All on her own, she'd found her perfect match.

12

"Go! Go! Go!" MARISSA shouted like a madwoman, leaping to her feet when Kyle got the puck late in the third period.

Eyes glued to the Phantoms' leading scorer and the sexiest man she'd ever met, she fisted her hands and willed him on as he flew down the ice. She might be leaving tomorrow, but she planned to root him on tonight.

Jammed into a sold-out arena among the home crowd rooting mostly for the other team, she held her breath as Kyle powered past the other players. She'd seen it throughout the game when he was on the ice. He was unbelievably fast. More than that, he could keep the puck under control as if he had glue on his stick. They called him the Playmaker with good reason.

Now, he drew back his stick for a breakaway shot. She could almost see the panic in the opposing goalie's eyes.

An opponent's stick came hurtling down out of nowhere, tomahawk-chopping Kyle's before he got the shot off. The home crowd roared in approval. The breakaway play died and the refs blew their whistles.

"Cheap shot!" Marissa called, hands cupped around her mouth as if that would megaphone the message to the offender. "You oversize goon! Did you see that?" she turned to the people seated nearby. "The other guy couldn't keep up so he flung his stick in the way."

Some Pittsburgh fans nearby chuckled at her, clearly proud of their team's goon. Kyle had explained to her before the game that some defenders resorted to cheap tactics to stop a goal, but she hadn't expected such violence. She'd never seen a live hockey game. The game riveted her. Or maybe it was just Kyle who fascinated her. She hadn't realized his incredible level of talent until tonight, seeing him compared to the rest of the players. He stood taller than all of them except his foster brother, his skills above and beyond the others on the ice.

"What's happening now?" she asked the fans around her, seeing the hockey rink erupt with tension. Players circled the refs, shouting at them and one another.

"Your guys aren't content with a hooking penalty," a helpful older woman explained to her from the seat to the right.

Kyle pulled off his gloves and threw them on the ice. From her position a few rows above rink-side she could see his expression and his body language—flexing jaw, lowered eyebrows, tense body. His power and strength were undeniable even as she feared what would come next.

The crowd was going wild now—stomping and banging their seats. Cheering on...what? Anger?

She was totally unprepared when the first fist flew. Even more unprepared to comprehend that it was Kyle doing the swinging. He'd gone after the defenseman who'd whacked his stick on the shot attempt. In the blink of an eye, Kyle's foster brother hit someone else, and soon it seemed as though the whole rink erupted in a brawl.

"Oh, no." She sank to her seat, hands pressed to her mouth.

Kyle had his opponent's jersey fisted in one hand while he used the other to hit. But since the defenseman outweighed him by about fifty pounds, the fight seemed bound to end badly for Kyle. Sure enough, a right-hand punch by the big man connected with Kyle's face, sending his head back and sending Marissa right out of her seat.

"Excuse me." Edging down the row past other fans' knees and cardboard trays of beers, Marissa reached the aisle.

Eyes glued to the ice, she watched as the refs finally pulled the fighters apart. Thank God.

Except instead of sending Kyle to the E.R. or even the locker room to tend to his head, they sent him to a little plastic cage they called the penalty box. Apparently in this game, you went to time-out for bad behavior. Didn't these refs have any idea what kind of damage a blow to the head could inflict? Thoughts of her mother's ordeal made her all the more anxious to make sure Kyle was okay.

The pressure in her chest told her exactly how scared she was for him. She didn't want to see him hurt. Didn't want to lose him. In fact, just thinking about it made her heart beat faster, almost as if...

She loved him.

Winding her way through the stands toward the section of seats containing the penalty box, she accidentally stepped on a sticky patch of trampled cotton candy, not looking where she was going. Could she possibly care so deeply about a man she'd just met?

The squeeze of her heart told her, absolutely yes. Maybe she was drawn to bigger-than-life personalities in spite of herself, her quieter nature responding to the confidence and charm of someone like Kyle. But beneath that bold exterior, Kyle shared her values, donating time to charity and staying out of the spotlight. He believed in hard work and discipline, his lifestyle far closer to hers than her jet-setting mother's.

"Can I help you, miss?" a grizzled usher asked her, his red shirt identifying him as staff.

He stood in front of a rope that closed off the step down to the seating section surrounding the penalty box.

"Can I get through here?" she asked, squinting to try to see Kyle, but he was hidden from view by fans for the home team shouting at him and knocking on the glass of the box where he sat.

An announcement about the penalties—one for each team—boomed over the P.A. system, drowning out the security guard's answer.

"Excuse me?" She leaned closer to the man, wishing Kyle would turn around and see her ten rows up. She still felt shaky with the realization that she cared for him far more than she ever thought she could feel about someone in such a short space of time.

Maybe her emotions were just running high after the draining months of taking care of her mom. No wonder her feelings were so close to the surface.

"Sorry miss, these are reserved seats. Season ticket holders only." He crossed his arms and resumed watching the action on the ice as play continued.

"But I'm Kyle's—" She paused, unsure how to finish that sentence. Girlfriend? Temporary diversion? Decoy mistress for the sake of the gossipmongers of the world?

What could she possibly be to him in the big scheme of things?

Stymied, she didn't know how to convince this sentry to let her pass.

"Marissa!" a feminine voice called to her over the din.

She didn't have to look far to spot the source. Two rows down in the forbidden season ticket-holder zone, Stacy Goodwell stood and waved both arms. Decked out in a fan sweater and a blue miniskirt that matched the base color in the team jersey, Stacy sat beside the man Marissa had researched for her: graphics microchip guru Isaac Reynolds. She recognized him from his pictures. He steadied Stacy during the enthusiastic waving, keeping her from toppling into the next row down with a hand at her waist.

"Down here!" Stacy cried, grinning ear to ear as Marissa spotted her.

"My friend really needs me," Marissa told the usher protecting the section, but he was already stepping aside for her, giving up the fight to keep Marissa out.

Or maybe the guy recognized Phil Goodwell's daughter. Goodwell owned the arenas in both Philadelphia and Pittsburgh as well as nearly a dozen others around the country. And for her part, Stacy was highly recognizable, with her asymmetrically cut platinum hair and a face so beautiful she could have graced a magazine cover.

But as Marissa made her way down the stairs toward Stacy and—more important—the penalty box, a horn blew and signaled the game was over. Instantly, the aisles filled with fans going the other way.

"I'll come to you!" Stacy called through the din, her hand waving over the top of the mob's collective heads. "Just a sec."

Marissa couldn't have argued if she tried. She tucked into the end of one row to get out of the way of people streaming up the stairs.

"I wanted to see if Kyle is okay," she explained to Stacy when she and her date reached the spot where Marissa stood. "He was in the penalty box."

"Well, he's out now!" Stacy hugged her, practically bubbling with a happiness that glowed. "We won!"

Had they? The score hardly registered with Marissa since she'd been so intent on seeing Kyle. Isaac moved toward them, sliding a protective arm around Stacy's waist.

"Stacy can get you downstairs where the players will be," Isaac informed her, his dark, serious gaze seeming to assess Marissa's deeper concern. "I'm Isaac, by the way."

"How rude of me," Stacy exclaimed, frowning. But she was already leading the way through the crowd.

Following, Marissa introduced herself to the man who'd inspired Stacy to make a huge, wholesale change in her life.

"Marissa Collins. It's a pleasure to meet you." She would have extended her hand, but they had to walk single file down a busy thoroughfare to keep up with Stacy's blond head as she bobbed and weaved through the crowd.

"I've heard a lot about you," Isaac told her, surprising her. "Although I hope Stacy won't have a need for your services any longer."

He said it so matter-of-factly that it took Marissa a moment to realize why. Isaac was staking claim to Stacy. She almost hadn't believed the two of them could be right for each other when she'd researched him. He'd sounded like a bit of a techno-geek when she'd read about everything he'd accomplished at such a young age. He held an honorary degree from MIT even though he'd left his studies early to take his first product to market.

But maybe Stacy's vibrant personality balanced his. Sometimes people sought partners with strengths they lacked. Isaac could help Stacy channel her talents and give her the direction and backbone she needed with her dad. Stacy would ensure the genius entrepreneur had a life outside his work.

"You know, a matchmaker can tell you how compatible you will be when you enter a new relationship," she remarked, already seeing how they'd fit together in the future. It was a service few people used, kind of like couple's counseling while you were still in the giddy stages of a new romance. She wanted to be certain this relationship would stick since Stacy deserved to be happy. "We can help you avoid common pitfalls and prepare you for—"

"We'll call you to set something up. I'm sure that would be helpful."

For a moment, Marissa forgot all about her need to get to Kyle. She was shocked that this man who'd only just met Stacy would agree so easily. If anything, women were generally more apt to agree to compatibility counseling. Men usually assumed they would conquer all obstacles as they arose. She halted in her steps to turn again and gauge his expression.

"Really?" She swayed forward as a woman with a crying toddler shoved past her to reach the exit. Would Kyle ever agree to something like that? Compatibility counseling by a more objective party?

She wondered if it would help them look beyond the things that kept them apart to the elements that could potentially hold them together.

"Stacy really respects your opinions." Isaac was a handsome man in a more unassuming way than Kyle Murphy's all-out good looks. There was something highly engaging about Isaac's insightfulness, and his shrewd, knowing gaze was smart without being smug. "I would be grateful if you could warn her what to expect with someone like me. She's happy now, but sometimes people tire of the very qualities that attract them in the first place."

Marissa started forward again, darting around a vendor rolling a pretzel cart, not wanting to lose Stacy in this crowd. And she really did need to see Kyle with her own eyes to assure herself he was okay. But first, the matchmaker in her couldn't resist finding out more about this intriguing relationship she had no part in crafting.

"You're genuinely thinking about a long-term future together, aren't you?" She didn't mean to put him on the spot, but it was obvious from the way he spoke about Stacy.

"In a world full of cynics, Stacy remains sweet and warmhearted. Completely unaffected. And for some unknown reason, she really digs me." He gave Marissa that quick flash of a grin again, but then he was looking up ahead, seeking out the woman who'd obviously captured his heart. "I know a stroke of good luck when I see it."

While Marissa mulled that over, Isaac pointed toward the right.

"She went this way," he informed her, making her realize she would have lost Stacy anyhow. "You have to get through security to reach the level with the locker rooms. But since Stacy's dad owns the joint, it shouldn't be a problem."

"Thank you." She hastened her step to catch up to Stacy, the crowd thinner here save for a few hard-core fans trying to convince the guards why they needed to be in the secured area.

It reminded Marissa of the groupies at her mother's concerts trying to wheedle a VIP backstage pass. As much as she wanted her mother to recover, Marissa realized she didn't miss the world that had come with touring. She'd personally played the secondary gate-keeper after the security guards for her mom—keeping lovesick fans out of the dressing room and telling pushy guys to take a hike.

Now that she thought about it, that's why she'd first bought her fake wedding band. It had been her decoy even then, when she'd been sixteen and guarding the superstar from men who would flirt with her to try to get past her.

"Isn't Isaac the greatest?" Stacy asked as Marissa reached her side.

They were waved through the doors while other fans bemoaned the unfairness of some people being allowed to enter and not others. Isaac stayed behind, telling Stacy he'd pick her up at the east gate whenever she was ready to leave.

"I like him," Marissa asserted, confident the guy had Stacy's best interests in mind. He wanted to make sure she was happy in the future. How thoughtful was that?

A little corner of her heart wished Kyle would look beyond the next game to think about her that way. She understood his drive and commitment, all the more after seeing him play. But bottom line, he wasn't at a point in his career where he would settle down.

"Can you believe I found him myself? I literally tripped on him. Oh, and that was after I tried to break into his van." Stacy pointed toward a big Phantoms logo on the outside of one of the locker room doors. Apparently the Philly team traveled with a full array of paraphenalia, right down to signage for the visiting-team locker room. "Kyle should be in there. I'll try to find someone to go in the he-man domain to get him for you."

While Stacy disappeared into an office, Marissa felt suddenly unsure. Should she bother him now? She'd been so worried about his head, but surely the team had sports trainers and medical staff who would look him over. Was she treading where she had no business? Amplifying her role in his life when they'd known from the start this was going to be temporary?

She and Kyle hadn't talked about compatibility counseling, as Isaac already had for himself and Stacy. When Marissa had reminded Kyle earlier today that neither one of them had wanted a relationship, he hadn't argued. Obviously, he still felt that way while she…

She'd fallen for him. For all her wisdom about matchmaking, and her awareness that she had no judgment about men when she was most attracted, she still made the same old mistakes.

Today, when Kyle had asked her to go on the road with him, at least she'd had the presence of mind not to jump on the offer. Spending more time with him would only dig her in deeper. She couldn't just leap into Kyle's world, traveling around the country with another superstar the way she had for so many years with Brandy Collins. She hadn't cared for that kind of life back then. Why would it be any different now, with a man who hadn't professed any kind of commitment toward her? She needed to remember she already had a huge commitment back home, to her mother.

"Harry can help you." Stacy returned, arm-in-arm with a gray-haired security guard who looked well past retirement age. "He'll find Kyle in the locker room to let him know you're here."

"Maybe I should just wait for him upstairs," Marissa demurred, already feeling out of place.

"Don't be silly," Stacy insisted, giving Harry's arm an urgent squeeze before she half dragged him toward the locker room. "Harry doesn't mind."

Too late to call him back, Marissa watched as the older man plowed through the locker room doors. Briefly, she could hear raised voices and shouting, a celebration inside for sure. That much, at least, gave her heart. They wouldn't be whooping it up over the play-off spot if one of their own was severely injured, right?

Still, she couldn't help but feel as though she'd just shown her hand too soon with Kyle Murphy. Revealed a bit too much about her feelings for him by chasing him down in his domain. But maybe it was just as well she was honest with him about getting in over her head. Because if her feelings for him weren't returned in some measure, if he wasn't ready for a more stable life and sense of commitment, she couldn't afford to indulge herself with the Phantoms' lauded playmaker anymore.

"JUST TWO MORE STITCHES," the team doctor assured Kyle as he lay on the gurney, his face half-sheathed in white paper to keep the area sterile while they worked on him.

"Good deal." He needed to shower and put in a quick appearance with the team to celebrate clinching their division. Mostly, he wanted to get off the table to see Marissa.

And wasn't that unexpected after how hard he'd worked to get here? The regimented training, the year-round discipline, the daily practices—all of it had been aimed at getting him to this moment, poised for the Stanley Cup play-offs. Yet the first thought in his head was the woman he'd just met, the woman who'd been a fixture in his thoughts from the moment he'd seen her.

And she was walking away from him tomorrow.

The realization burned more than the doctor's needle in his skin.

"Kyle Murphy?" an unfamiliar voice cackled from the doorway while the assisting doc tied off the face embroidery.

"Right here." Kyle lifted a hand to assure the old guy he'd found the correct party, his knuckles taped and bandaged since he'd split them open. In his peripheral version, he saw a gray-haired security guard.

"I've got a couple of ladies looking for you." The man hitched at pants that were a size too big for his thin frame. "Marissa someone or other. You know her?"

"Yes." He swiped off the surgical paper and sat up too fast, his jaw throbbing harder. "Where is she?"

"Just outside the main entrance to the visitors' locker room," the old-timer answered, adjusting the visor of his uniform cap. "We caught a lucky break stopping your goal at the end, son. You clinched your division, but Pittsburgh is still scrapping for every extra point to nab a wildcard slot."

Standing, Kyle thanked the medical staff and left the smell of antiseptic to move into the hallway with the security guard.

"Didn't feel like a lucky break when your goon nearly took my arm off with that hack before the hooking call." Kyle understood an occasional hit. What had ticked him off was that the blow to the stick hit his wrist, as well. A wrist injury at this point could finish his season.

"He's a rough one," the guard admitted as he led Kyle past the visiting team offices toward the exit. "But your enforcer got a few licks in tonight, too. Did you see the hip check Rankin gave number ten after you went in the box? Your brother can rumble with the best of 'em."

"Gotta have someone watching my back." Kyle grinned before he remembered the stitches and promptly straightened his face. "Damn, that's sore."

The older man chuckled as he tugged open the locker room double doors. "Good luck in the play-offs, son. Your lady friend is right out here."

Kyle's eyes landed on Marissa. Her arms were folded and a stiff, square purse dangled from her arm on a chain strap. Her low heels and Capri pants looked like something Marilyn Monroe would have worn on the weekends. Marissa's white blouse sported a Phantoms pin on one pocket, the small nod to his team all the sweeter since he'd bet she wouldn't normally wear fan paraphernalia.

He warmed inside just looking at her. And not just because of the attraction. He liked having her here, knowing that someone cared if he got a few teeth knocked out or needed stitches. In a family full of brothers, you learned to toughen up in a hurry, because the TLC quota was limited. Feeling that tenderness from Marissa had been nice.

How could he convince her to stay?

"Marissa." He wanted to wrap her in his arms, but he remembered he hadn't showered and he wasn't sure what her reaction would be. He still wore hockey shorts and pads on his legs, but someone had helped strip off his jersey before he'd gone in to get his face sewn up.

And while she'd seen him when he'd been half-naked and sweating before, the circumstances had been very, very different.

"Ahem." Near Marissa, someone cleared her throat. Kyle looked to see a pretty blonde with wide blue eyes that matched all the blue Phantoms gear she wore, right down to a knitted scarf flung around her neck. "I'll just leave you two alone."

Kyle nodded to the mystery woman as she walked away, surprised he hadn't even noticed her standing there at first. Marissa had stolen his focus in a big way.

"Are you okay?" Marissa stepped closer, her eyes on his injury and her face so pale he wondered if the sight of blood bothered her.

"It's nothing," he assured her. "The hits look worse than they are."

She blinked up at him, some of the color returning to her cheeks.

"It's never healthy to have your head snapped back to that degree." She reached up to cup his face by the temples, carefully avoiding his jaw. "Did they do a concussion test?"

He realized she was staring intently at his pupils and he guessed she was taking a test of her own.

"Marissa, I'm fine." He took her hands in his, freeing her from any nursing obligations. "My brothers hit harder than that wimp Wolfson. Why don't I go clean up and I'll meet you in the team lounge? You and your friend can grab something to eat while you wait."

He didn't mention anything about finding her a flight home, just in case she'd changed her mind. Just in case he could pull out a last-minute miracle—the ultimate play for a guy who was known for competing until the last second.

She nodded stiffly, agreed too readily, when he could tell by her body language that she was upset.

"What's wrong?" he asked, unable to go back and party with his team when Marissa seemed so distant. "Is it your mom? Is everything okay back home?"

"Her condition is the same. She starts the new treatment tomorrow thanks to you. We'll be okay." As he clutched the chain of her purse strap as if it was a lifeline, her white knuckles told him a different story.

Damn it. She still wanted to leave. He could feel it in the tension between them.

"Then what is it? Something's wrong and I can't go back in there and pretend to be thrilled about a playoff spot when I know you're upset." Seeing one of his teammates come tearing out into the hallway with a bottle of champagne in hand, Kyle grabbed Marissa's hand and tugged her into an empty office behind them.

He closed the door before they were spotted, shutting them into a cramped ten-by-ten room with a desk, chair and a landline. It seemed no one on the Phantoms had claimed the space for the night, as the desk was free of paperwork.

"What are you doing?" Marissa's violet eyes searched his from behind her tortoiseshell glasses. "You should celebrate your big victory."

She carefully avoided a bag full of new pucks that

looked like promo items for a future giveaway day at the arena.

"It doesn't feel like a victory." He should be thrilled. Shaking champagne all over Axel's head until the big Finn gave in and drank a few drops. "I feel like my team just got shut out. Like I'm on the verge of the biggest loss yet. Why is that?"

A relationship was new ground for him, but he wanted a win with Marissa, too.

He cleared away the big, old-fashioned telephone on the aluminum desk, took a seat on the surface and pulled her between his legs. He wanted to be able to look her in the eye.

"This isn't a good time—"

"There's nothing more important to me right now than you." He cupped her shoulders, absorbed the feel of her through her cotton blouse. "Is it the fight? I don't usually get ticked off like that, but the guy hacked at my shooting wrist."

"It's not just that," she admitted, though her wording suggested the fight played a role. "I guess I'm struggling with being a backstage presence again. Seeing you get hurt tonight made me realize I could go right back to being a caretaker, the practical detail person who helps someone else achieve their dreams without ever discovering my own."

Honestly, the blow from Wolfson hadn't been nearly as out-of-the-blue as this one was. Kyle thought he might have reeled a little more from it, too.

"I don't need a caretaker." Where the hell had she ever gotten that idea? The desk beneath him squeaked as he leaned forward to impress his point, his hands running down the length of her arms. "I've been on the road on my own since my college career—"

"You're right. That's not the best word." She set her boxy purse on the table beside him, not seeming to mind the sweaty smell of him. "But whether you want someone on the road to care for you or not, I already do. I *care*. And I can't invest all of myself in that kind of relationship without a mutual commitment."

"And I want to make one." He squeezed her hands in his, more certain than ever that he needed to be with her.

That got her attention. She practically did a double take.

"Excuse me?" Her soft words were half drowned out by the din in the locker room next door. Guys hooting and hollering, banging lockers and generally going nuts over a big victory.

"I want to commit to you, Marissa. I want a relationship." It was a big-as-hell step for him. A grown-up step. But all the reasons he hadn't wanted a relationship in the past didn't apply with her. "You're not some fly-by-night girlfriend who's going to get lonely while I'm on the road and mess around behind my back. You care about the same things I do. You're loyal. Traditional. Hell, I think your job alone qualifies you as a romantic. And I love that."

Her lower lip dropped, shock rounding her mouth in a silent response.

"We have something special here," he pressed. "You know it. Let's not overthink it before it even gets off the ground, okay? Why not take a chance and see how amazing we can be together?"

_13_

ANY OTHER WOMAN WOULD be turning cartwheels. _She_ should be turning cartwheels.

Marissa remembered Kyle had dismissed the idea of a relationship out of hand just days ago. And now, he wanted to make a commitment to her. But no matter what he wanted, the practical side of her couldn't envision how it could ever work.

"I am a romantic," she agreed. "But that doesn't mean I'm willing to ignore all the obvious problems in the hope of a few months of fun and passion. I won't tilt at windmills, no matter how much I would like things to work between us."

Next door, his team burst into some kind of cheer for the coach, toasting him and practically shaking the walls with male shouts and laughter. In the office, the sweat cooled on Kyle's bare chest, his strong, delectable body only a small facet of what attracted her to him. She probably should have turned and run when she'd been too speechless to order her drink that first night they'd met.

Yet she couldn't find it in her heart to regret the time they'd spent together since then.

He looked at her now with dawning realization in his eyes. She hadn't given him the answer he'd hoped for, and she could almost see him closing off from her. Shutting down. His hands slid from hers. A part of her wanted to take back her words and simply enjoy whatever time she could have with him.

"May I ask what you think the obvious problems are?" His voice sounded like a stranger's and she felt her heart crack down the center.

She was going to lose him.

"Your commitment is to hockey," she reminded him, knowing the sport would always come first for him until he won the trophy he wanted so badly. "Mine is to my mother, at least until she recovers. We've known that all along."

"Are you honestly asking me to give up hockey to make a commitment to you?"

Slowly, she shook her head. "I know better than that. I wouldn't expect you to walk away from the game any more than you'd want me to leave my mom to recover on her own."

She braced herself, waiting for his reply. And her heart broke a little more when he said nothing. A brief, accepting nod was his only response.

Her knees felt liquid and shaky. Her heart raced and she worried she'd do something humiliating like sob her eyes out if she stayed there any longer. So, darting forward for one last kiss on his cheek, she tried not to think about all she was giving up. All she would be leaving behind.

"I'm sorry," she said, picking up her purse before she walked out of the office and out of his life.

KYLE PLAYED THE WORST game of his career in Tampa two days later. Then, after a crappy couple of days back in Philadelphia, he'd played an even worse game against Ottawa to end the regular season. The Phantoms were headed to the play-offs, but he was playing like garbage.

Now, a week after he and Marissa had said goodbye, he fumed silently on the flight home from Ottawa. He jammed his headphones on his ears—the big-ass, noise cancelling kind—and cranked up the tunes, determined not to talk to anyone on the team's late flight back to Philadelphia. He'd taken a seat in the last row, keeping his bag beside him to advertise that he didn't want company.

The game hadn't been as important since they'd already secured the play-off spot. At this point, they were playing for higher seeding and the benefit of home-ice advantage in the upcoming weeks. So the games still mattered. And Kyle had choked.

He'd missed a breakaway shot—no excuse of a hooking penalty this time. Missed a pass from Ax that should have been a clear-cut assist. His crap level of play was bringing down his brother, his coach, his whole team.

Of course, this was all because of Marissa. She had him so turned around he couldn't begin to know what had gone wrong there. She'd said that relationships— caring too much—messed with her perspective. He'd brushed off that comment at the time, not giving it much weight. But her refusal to see room for a compromise sure felt like a wrong-headed perspective to him. Why couldn't they find some middle ground—with her need to be with her mom and his desire to have her with him? He'd given ground by agreeing to make a commitment to her. What about her? Still, feeling "right" didn't soothe the hole in his gut that had been burning ever since she'd left.

A shift in the seat beside him made him open his eyes and glare at whoever had intruded in his personal space. Ax. No surprise there. When had the Finn ever respected a boundary?

Pissed and in no mood to talk about it, Kyle kept his earphones in place.

Of course, that just resulted in Axel yanking the things off, letting them drop down to Kyle's neck.

"What gives?" Ax asked without prelude.

"I don't know what you're talking about."

"You're playing like you have a boulder on your back and you're sending off a vibe like you'll kill the next teammate who asks you about it." Axel glared, the U-shaped scar on his face an angry red line. "That girl you liked. The one who wore the wedding ring. Did she end up married, after all?"

Cursing the bold and unapologetic nosiness of family, Kyle kept the music on so he could at least play the drum solo on his knees. Too bad it wasn't the same with the music wafting up from the earphones now ringing his neck.

"Marissa. And no, she's not married. She just doesn't want to be with me. End of story."

"The end of the bullshit version, maybe. Why don't you tell me the real one?"

A flight attendant came around with a meal, a welcome bonus of the team plane since commercial flights would just as soon starve their customers. Seated on the aisle, Ax got trays for both of them while the younger guys tossed a beach ball around the seats up front.

Kyle would probably knock the thing into the next century if it came his way. He was in that kind of mood. Instead, he concentrated on his salmon, forking it down in record time.

"Okay, let me guess," Axel said finally, when no information was forthcoming. "You hit a snag and trotted out the line about no relationships during the play-offs. She thought it was bogus and wanted a relationship, so she walked."

"I would have been in better shape if I'd stuck to my guns about no relationships during the play-offs." Maybe he could have simply seen her around town when the team played at home. Taken her out for dinner or back to his place.

Except she didn't want any part of a half-ass commitment, and she wouldn't compromise enough to really make a full-blown relationship work.

"You wanted a relationship?" Ax asked, zeroing in on the heart of the matter in no time.

But then, they'd been friends since they were old enough to date. They'd both faced the same problem of investing everything into a demanding sport, which didn't leave much time for developing meaningful relationships. Just look at how many guys on the team struggled with divorce. It wasn't a lifestyle many women would sign on for.

"I was open to it," Kyle replied cautiously, knowing this interrogation wasn't going to end until he told Ax enough to satisfy him.

"And she wasn't?" Axel's fork fell from his fingers as he peered over at Kyle and snapped off the iPod still blaring at full volume through the fallen headphones.

"She's confused." Kyle couldn't begin to understand why or how things had gotten so muddled for her. "She's got a mother with a traumatic brain injury, and when it comes down to it, she doesn't want to be on the road all the time."

"No surprise there, right?" Axel went back to shoveling in his food. "We'd be the same way with your mom."

"Yeah, but—"

"What? You can work around that, can't you? Spend summers in Philadelphia. You can fly back to Philly on the off days during the road trips, as well. It's not like you're a rookie anymore. Coach would let you go."

"Right. Except she didn't even make that an option. She said she won't give up her mom and I won't give up hockey, so see you around. Don't let the door hit you on your way out. That kind of thing."

Axel kept eating. "You just let her walk away like it was over?"

"What are you, the effing team fortune-teller now?" He shoved aside his tray. "How do you know what happened?"

A few heads turned from the seats in front of them.

Obviously, he'd raised his voice. But Kyle was too ticked off to rein it in.

"I *don't* know. I'm asking you, Murph. Did you fall for this girl and then just throw your hands in the air when it got rough after...what? A few days?"

"She was the one who didn't want to try, bro. Not me."

"You know what your problem is?" Axel pointed a finger in his face, a ballsy move when Kyle was already walking a razor's edge in this mood. "Everything comes easy to you. Do you know how hard the rest of the world has to work to accomplish things you take for granted?"

The rest of the conversations on the plane grew noticeably quieter. A few of the veterans popped in their own headphones, knowing better than to get involved, but the rookies had their heads on a swivel to see what was happening.

"You're kidding me, right?" Kyle removed the finger from his face, careful to keep his movements dispassionate so the coach couldn't accuse them of fighting. "You're going to spout off to me now when I just had the worst game of my life and my girl left me?"

Yeah, at this point, discretion was no longer at the top of his list.

"In your worst game, you still had a goal and an assist. How do you think it makes Matthias over there feel—" he pointed to a rookie who hadn't even dressed for the game "—when you piss and moan about your missed shots when he'd give his eyeteeth to score at this level? You're freaking gifted, man. From racing sailboats on the Cape to backyard football with your brothers, you kick everyone's ass in any sport you try. So when an obstacle comes your way, do you even have any clue what to do about it?"

Somewhere in that little rant, some of Kyle's anger seeped away. Possibly about the time Ax said he was gifted, whatever the hell that meant.

"You know that's not true. Remember how I almost failed Advanced Finance?" They'd been college roommates, spending far more time on the ice than they had in the classroom.

"Because you got a girlfriend that semester."

That was true, now that he thought about it. The class would have been a cakewalk if he'd actually attended.

"I busted my butt to make up for all that material I missed." He worked hard then and he worked hard now. Didn't he?

Around them, the noise level on the plane picked back up again now that the possibility of a blowout seemed to have passed. Kyle grappled with the idea that he was a stranger to hard work when he'd devoted hours and hours and whole off-seasons to perfecting what he did best.

Then again, Axel wasn't the kind of guy to start trouble for no reason. Kyle knew him better than that. Ax wouldn't say it if he didn't think there was some truth to it.

"I know, man. And you make a hell of a lot with what you've been given. But even with women, you don't have a lot of experience putting in the time to make a relationship successful. I tried it once and it was tough."

Standing, Axel clapped him on the shoulder and cleared the trays away, taking them to the flight attendant at the front of the plane. Probably walking away from the conversation for good.

Leaving Kyle to wonder if he should rethink what had happened with Marissa. He couldn't quit hockey. She hadn't even asked him to. But maybe, if he dug deeper and worked harder, he could figure out more viable alternatives. Help Marissa see a way that she could be with him and still take care of her mom.

Because being without her now made him realize exactly how much he'd come to care about her. How much he wanted things to work out with her. He'd known even before the game in Pittsburgh that she was too important to let slip away, but he'd gone and done just that.

Sliding his earphones back into place, he turned up the music feeling less like he wanted to hit something and more like he wanted to fix something. He could do the hard work, whether Ax knew it or not.

How would he ever run a successful youth hockey camp if he couldn't muster strength off the ice as well as on?

Besides, Marissa Collins was worth bringing his A-game.

Now all he had to do was figure out what it would take to win back a traditional, romantic woman....

"Mom?" Marissa placed her hand on her mother's shoulder, careful to wake her slowly. "You have a visitor."

Brandy Collins had been taking her new treatment

for six days. The doctors had warned Marissa not to expect miracles. But she was just grateful to try something different after months of seeing little progress. How could she live with herself if she hadn't exhausted every possible avenue for her mother's full recovery?

Now, with Stacy and Isaac waiting a few feet away in the dining room of the big, old house that had been Brandy's home for the past ten years, Marissa watched as her mother lifted her eyelids.

"Hey, baby girl," she said softly, the endearment falling easily from her lips as if she recognized Marissa immediately. Her famous voice sounded scratchy from sleep.

"Mom?" Marissa felt a pang in her chest, the fresh stab of hope almost painful after all this time of waiting for any sign of improvement. And her heart was all the more tender in the wake of her breakup with Kyle, her emotions all over the place.

Could she trust herself now—trust her belief that she'd just seen genuine awareness in her mom's eyes? Or was she simply desperate for some sign of healing?

"Thank you." Her mother reached awkwardly for Marissa's hand and squeezed it. Her eyes were clear and focused. Almost disconcertingly cognizant. "Thank you, baby."

Marissa's knees wobbled. They might have gone out from under her if Isaac and Stacy hadn't swooped in to steady her. Adrenaline buzzed while the pair bracketed her, Stacy with a huge bouquet of local wildflowers and Isaac with a new CD of a classic seventies band that Brandy had frequently cited in interviews as one of her all-time favorites.

Was this the moment Marissa had been waiting for?

"Ms. Collins?" Stacy ventured. "How do you feel?"

Brandy blinked. Shook her head as if trying to clear it. When she opened her eyes again, that flash of recognition had vanished. The skin between her brows wrinkled as if she were trying to pull back a memory that wouldn't come.

It was an expression that Marissa had seen on her mother's face innumerable times over the past few months. The letdown was sharp, leaving her feeling deflated. Numb.

But there'd been a hopeful moment, right? Her throat closed around a lump, her eyes burning.

"It's okay, Mom." Marissa rubbed her mom's arm to comfort her. And herself. "You're getting better."

She had to believe that. Her faith in her mother's ability to heal had driven her through months of caregiving. But it had zapped her emotional reserves more than she'd realized, leaving her little to offer a great guy when he came along.

Brandy stared at her for a long moment, before her eyes moved to Stacy. She smiled and reached for the bouquet of wildflowers while Marissa tried to recover herself.

"One step forward, two steps back," she whispered to herself, knowing that recovery would take time.

But she would be there beside her through it all, even if had cost her…so much. Would she look back one day and wonder "what if?" Regret that she hadn't tried to make things work with Kyle? In many ways she already did.

"Marissa?" Isaac set the CD on her mother's bedside

and moved back a step while Stacy told Brandy Collins all about her new video blog. "Can I talk to you?"

It had been sweet of them to visit, although Marissa guessed Stacy wanted to check up on her after the way she'd lit out of Pittsburgh as if the hounds of hell were at her heels. And they were, sort of. They were named Heartache and Regret, and they bit with a vengeance. But even after a week away from Kyle, she didn't have any answers for the problems that kept her apart from him.

Now, she moved back a step from her mother's bed, praying that she hadn't just dreamed the flash of recognition she'd seen in her mom's eyes after all this time. Maybe the new experimental treatments would help.

"Sure." Marissa picked up a silver water pitcher she'd filled for the guests, ice clanking against the sides. "Can I get you anything to drink?"

"That'd be great." Isaac took a glass and waited for her to fill her own. He looked around the dining room filled with her mother's things. "You must have worked hard to convert this space to accommodate your mom."

She smiled at the guitars hanging on the walls. The photographs filling every free space.

"If you ever want me to film the room for you and digitize it, we could project the surroundings for her somewhere else, so you could move her anywhere you wanted."

"Excuse me?" She knew she was sensitive about her mom and the choices she'd made about her mother's care, so she tried not to let the comment ruffle her feathers.

Kyle had suggested something similar and she hadn't

been ready to consider it. Now, Isaac sipped his water and gestured to the bank of windows overlooking the spring gardens.

"I'm in the graphics business. And we're improving 3-D technology and multimedia mapping daily, ensuring people don't have to wear glasses to enjoy a more fully developed environment. I could recreate the look of this room somewhere else if that would prove helpful to you. You know, if you think your mother would be more comfortable in a real bedroom, for example, instead of the dining room. I could film her current surroundings and set up a three-dimensional image—"

"Really?" She frowned even though she could immediately perceive the benefit of such a plan. She hadn't wanted to sell the house because the doctors said familiar surroundings might anchor her mother. But it sure tied her hands when it came to paying for the expensive in-home care visits from any number of medical professionals.

"Easily. The new technology I have coming out is top secret until I get it to market, but I could make it available to you. It would look extremely convincing." Isaac reached for the CD he'd brought and popped it in a player near the water pitcher. "I can come back with some equipment today, if you want."

Marissa's chest tightened again. It was kind of Stacy and Isaac to come in the first place. Visitor traffic had died off months ago. But it was even more kind of Isaac to offer his expertise and a tool to aid in her mother's recovery.

She'd resisted moving her mom to a rehab facility, where patients were limited on how much they could bring. There'd be no room for her prized possessions. But if at least some of the environment was virtual, she wouldn't have to hang priceless guitars on the walls of a medical institution. Her mother could have access to more immediate care while still benefiting from the comfort of familiar surroundings, surroundings that could help bring back lost memories and maintain a connection with her past.

If Marissa had known about this before, might she have been less inclined to push Kyle away? Certainly it would have opened up some more options for traveling. But then, maybe she'd allowed herself to be scared off from a relationship too easily. She'd been afraid of the knowledge that she'd loved him, for one thing. While she'd made peace with living in her mother's shadow long ago, she hadn't necessarily wanted to reciprocate that dynamic with Kyle. He was a superstar. A strong, talented, amazing man.

And instead of being a strong woman for him, she'd scurried away like a twit, too scared to embrace the possibility of a future for fear she'd end up hurt.

If her mom recovered right now, she'd tell Marissa to stop being a coward. Her eyes went to the other side of the room where her mom lay. She wondered what other advice her mother might give.

Don't you dare hide behind me, young lady!

The words, so vivid in Marissa's mind, and yet sounding distinctly like Brandy Collins when she was all fired up, set Marissa back on her heels. Where had that idea come from? By the look of her mom nodding vaguely at something Stacy was saying, Marissa knew Brandy hadn't uttered them.

They were probably a truth she'd known deep in her heart all along—that she occasionally took shelter from her own life in the shadow of her mom's, complicit in the helper role she'd always gravitated toward. She couldn't use her mother's injury as a reason not to take chances. Maybe she needed to take more responsibility for carving out the kind of life she wanted to have with Kyle instead of waiting for the ideal situation.

Wouldn't she rather have an ideal man?

Tears threatened, and she didn't think she could hold them back.

"Uh—Stacy?" Isaac called, apparently seeing the imminent waterworks. "You'd better come here."

"It's nothing," Marissa insisted, not wanting the whole room to watch her weep. But her voice came out squeaky, advertising her emotions all too well.

She'd watched Kyle's games on TV since she'd left Pittsburgh. He'd played well for an average player, but she knew it wasn't his top form. Guilt had pinched her, as she knew he was feeling her loss as much as she was missing him. But not until today had she realized how little effort she'd made to work things out with him. Isaac had offered her a small piece of the puzzle—a way to start compromising with Kyle toward a more workable relationship.

But recognizing how emotionally depleted she'd been—running on empty to try to hold her life and her mom's together—also made a big impact. It hadn't occurred to her that she wasn't making the best decisions now, not until she'd felt the deep disappointment after seeing Brandy look at her with recognition for only those few precious moments.

Footsteps clicking across the hardwood alerted her to Stacy joining them.

"Holy moly!" She picked up her pace when she saw Marissa and then frowned at Isaac. "I left you alone for two minutes and you made her cry?" She put an arm around Marissa. "Isaac, you should bring the dogs in from the kitchen. Tink and Belle will cheer her up."

"That's okay," Marissa protested, smiling. "I'm fine. Isaac gave me a great idea. And helped me realize I made a big mistake with Kyle."

14

MARISSA COLLINS WAS IN the market for a man, a tall, dark and gorgeous man. In fact, she'd set her sights on Philadelphia's most wanted eligible bachelor.

And this time, she planned to keep the prize catch for herself.

She wove through the partygoers on the patio of a historic Philadelphia hotel, a few patio heaters employed to ward off the chill lingering in the April air. But this was a hockey-going crowd, come to celebrate the city's division champs, so they didn't mind a little bite to the breeze. Marissa wore a vintage smoking jacket over her wide-legged trousers, channeling her inner Katherine Hepburn. She could use a little of that Hepburn grit tonight.

In the pocket of her jacket, her cell phone vibrated against her thigh. She never would have heard it, since a DJ played rock-and-roll classics well loved by the locals. She paused by a low brick wall that wrapped around a seating area to retrieve the call. No, the text.

Have u seen him yet?

Stacy must be trolling the crowd, too, both of them

in search of Kyle. And if Stacy had attended the event, Isaac must be here, too, as the two of them had been charmingly inseparable ever since they'd met. Stacy had convinced Isaac to help with the filming and editing of *Diva No More*—the visual component was his area of expertise with his graphics background. She'd insisted he needed more fun and balance in his life after the years of nonstop work on honing his graphics chip. Now the video blog had a look that was polished and edgy at the same time, with supporting parts shot in black and white, edited into Stacy's irrepressible narrative.

In turn, Isaac had convinced Stacy to film an upcoming edition with a reunion between her and her father, a moment Phil Goodwell was apparently excited about since he grudgingly approved of Isaac Reynolds. He might not have Kyle's superstar athlete appeal or the Murphy family connections, but Isaac's business clout was undeniable, and greedy Goodwell would surely find a way to make the most of it. Mostly, Marissa was just happy that Isaac would help Stacy find a way to keep a relationship with her dad while maintaining a few barriers, too. And she liked the idea that Goodwell wouldn't try anything petty like withholding funds from Kyle's Full Strength Hockey Camp now that he understood he couldn't dictate Stacy's life.

Compatibility counseling for that pair was becoming a moot point in Marissa's opinion, but Isaac still planned to give the session to Stacy for a birthday gift next month—right after the spa day he'd booked for her. Because no matter how much independence Stacy carved out for herself, she would always have a diva side. Marissa couldn't help but admire how Stacy had found a niche for herself, an arena where she thrived.

Maybe Marissa could do the same—be there for her mother, but protect a part of her life that was all her own.

Nada, she texted back, peering around the milling crowd made up mostly of season ticket holders but also a few random fans who'd won local contests for the chance to attend the high-end soiree. Proceeds would benefit a Phantoms' charity.

Marissa was nervous about seeing him, even though she had rehearsed what she'd say. She was like a junior-high girl waiting to ask a boy to dance. And damn it, where had her inner Katherine Hepburn gone?

Have you checked the bar?

Marissa pocketed the phone, thinking that would be the coincidence of all coincidences. The night already felt like déjà vu, between the high-end party and the hockey team strengthening community ties with an out-reach event. It felt like the night they'd met. The night she'd tried to land Kyle for another woman and wound up falling for him herself.

No way would he be working the bar again.

Unless…did Stacy know something she didn't?

Spinning toward the nearest outdoor counter serving drinks, Marissa saw a young woman with an apron and a ponytail pouring red wine from a decanter. No dice. So, turning in the other direction, she trekked through a few groups of fans and Phantoms' corporate sponsors to find another bar. Night had fallen, though, and despite the lanterns burning around the courtyard garden, she couldn't see who was serving the drinks.

Whoever it was, he had quite a crowd. She guessed that meant either a juggling bartender was putting on a show with the bottles, or a player had taken over the post to mingle with his admirers.

Butterflies took flight in her belly, a fluttery feeling that made her breathe faster. It had to be him.

"Excuse me." She tried to pass a hulking guy twice her size, but her words didn't carry high enough to the giant's ears over the doo-wop song playing. "Excuse me," she tried again.

When the giant turned, she recognized Kyle's foster bother, Axel Rankin, from the game she'd seen in Pittsburgh. And, of course, the games she'd watched at home on her TV when the Phantoms played in Tampa Bay and Ottawa. Marissa was reading up on hockey in her spare time and now understood the positions better.

"Hello, Axel," she said, extending her hand. "I'm Marissa Collins, Kyle's…friend."

The big guy was already shaking her hand.

"Nice to meet you," he returned politely, keeping her hand and tugging her closer to guide her through the crowd. "Let me get you a drink. The crowd is starting to really pile in."

"Um…" She noticed Axel didn't have any trouble bypassing the guests circling the bar. "Okay."

Axel got pats on the back and cheers wherever he went. People raised their glasses and wished him good luck in the play-offs.

"Congratulations on making it to the play-offs." She turned toward his ear and arched up on her toes to say it, hoping the message made it a foot above her head. "You're the man of the hour."

"Yeah, me and twenty-two other guys. Thanks." He shouldered by another player who was next in line and deposited Marissa behind him.

Where she couldn't see a thing thanks to another massive set of shoulders. Damn it. Was Kyle really up there?

She turned to apologize to whoever she'd cut off in the line and found Stacy Goodwell grinning ear to ear.

"Hi." She gave a little wave, but didn't hug Marissa right away. Which seemed strange until Marissa realized she was on camera. "Act natural," Stacy stage-whispered.

Isaac stood beside the line, filming them with a small, handheld camera.

"What's going on?" Marissa asked, stepping outside the line to try to see around the player in front of her.

Too bad Axel was right there crowding in front of her. Honestly, was this some kind of conspiracy? She adjusted her glasses on her nose and tried not to let them rattle her. Pivoting to Stacy and Isaac, she prepared to squeeze the answers out of her friends when...

"Can I help you?"

The familiar baritone rumbled, warm and engaging. Just the way it had the first time she'd heard Kyle's voice. The crowd had magically thinned between her and the bar. Axel Rankin and the player who'd been blocking her view had both disappeared. She now stood face-to-face with the man she loved. The man who'd rendered her absolutely speechless the first time she'd looked at him.

He watched her now, green eyes alert as if he was studying an opponent he needed to watch carefully.

The gash on his jaw remained red, but the stitches were gone and the swelling had diminished.

"Seltzer over ice," she blurted, forgetting all about the words she'd rehearsed. The practical, well-reasoned plan for why they could still make this work.

"Seltzer on the rocks coming up." He took his time getting out the bottle, ignoring the line behind her.

Actually, Axel came to the rescue then, entering the spot behind the bar next to Kyle and calling for the next in line.

Kyle and Marissa shifted down to the end of the serving station while he poured her drink. Beside her, Marissa heard Stacy order a wine spritzer as she chatted with Isaac, so Marissa guessed that her awkward apology to Kyle wouldn't end up on a new edition of *Diva No More,* thank goodness.

"How have you been?" she asked Kyle while he turned to put the ice in the glass.

"My stats are down but the rest of the team is playing well. Ax has had a goal in each of the last two games now that he's not feeding me the puck all the time. I'm happy for him." He passed Axel a bottle of vodka from underneath the counter, apparently tuned in to whatever the next patron had requested.

"I'm sorry if I had anything to do with… That is, I'm sorry for what happened in Pittsburgh." She twisted the chain on her purse, hoping she would have the chance to explain that she'd been emotionally burned out and not thinking clearly.

What if he shut her down without hearing her out? What if he'd already moved on? The thought made her stomach knot, the butterfly fluttering turning to cold dread.

"I was having a lot of fun until you bailed out on me." He handed her the seltzer in a champagne flute, the bubbles still fizzing high above the rim.

He took his time pouring a matching glass—for him?—making her wonder if he might join her for a drink. Heaven knew, Axel looked plenty capable of taking over the bartending duties as he flirted with an elderly lady, putting extra cherries in her Coke.

"I think I might have had a panic attack," she admitted. "Or maybe I was just overwrought seeing you get hurt. And while I don't want to make excuses—" she moved her purse off the bar after another woman put her elbow on it "—I suspect the stress from losing the matchmaking gig and trying to find a way to help my mom had been eating away at me for a while. So I panicked with you."

"It probably wouldn't have been healthy to be with a guy who made you worry so much." He dropped a couple of ice cubes in his own drink.

She swallowed hard, thinking this wasn't going well at all.

"You don't." She reached over the bar, her hand landing on his forearm. "I wouldn't. That is, you're not the one who causes all the stress. I realized that taking care of my mom has taken a toll, but I'm working with Isaac to—"

"Who the hell is Isaac?" He straightened and she recognized the posture from the moment he'd thrown off his gloves that night on the ice in Pittsburgh.

Could he be jealous? A wishful part of her heart hoped it was so.

"He designs graphics chips. And he's the new boyfriend of my former client. The client responsible for us meeting, by the way. She's turned a new leaf and left her father's controlling ways behind." Marissa was so proud of Stacy, and so grateful to her, too. "Stacy Goodwell has been instrumental in helping Isaac—the chip maker—film my mother's house for a new 3-D visual environment that will make it easier for me to move her to a safer, staffed facility."

The decision had been difficult in spite of the new technology Isaac had offered. But after discussing it with Brandy's doctors and weighing the benefits of both options, they'd all agreed the change might be beneficial to Brandy's recovery.

Kyle lifted his brows.

"Do you want to have a seat?" He gestured to a row of tables tucked against the historic hotel some distance from the band and the mayhem. Only two of the four were taken; the rest of the crowd was on their feet.

"I'd love that," she admitted, grateful to have some time alone with him. Well, alone amidst five hundred other people.

"You're moving your mom?" He carried both their glasses, bending his head in her direction so he could hear her response.

The intimacy of the gesture warmed her. Made her feel like part of a couple again.

"I realized, with the help of friends, that I may have been using the excuse of taking care of her to hide from taking chances." She'd done a lot of soul-searching during a long, hard week. "And not just since the accident. Since always. She's never demanded anything from me. I just gravitate toward the helper roles. I'm good at them."

Reaching a wrought-iron table near a patio heater that warmed a small ring of air around them, Kyle pulled a chair out for her.

While she took a seat, he settled their glasses on the table and stole a candle from a nearby empty table to put on theirs, casting them in a golden glow.

"You know, I understand if you want to achieve dreams of your own and explore other career options. But I also know there's nothing wrong with being there for your friends and your mom. Your clients. Helping people find love and happiness is important. Something to be proud of."

His words touched her.

"I guess I don't think about it like that, but I should."

"Damn right you should. Bringing two people together…that's a whole hell of a lot more special than hoisting the Stanley Cup. But we all have to play to our own strengths, right?"

A lump formed in her throat and she had to bite her lip before she could speak.

"Thank you." She reached for his hand across the table, needing to touch him to make her case. "Kyle, I know I have a habit of putting up barriers with everything from my glasses and my matchmaking questionnaires to fake wedding bands and excuses for how a relationship could never work. But they are all total B.S., and I know that now."

She took a deep breath, needing to continue before she lost the head of steam.

"I actually… I'm falling for you." The magnitude of the gamble made her head feel as fuzzy as the seltzer still fizzing away in the glass beside her. "I realized it after you got hit that night in Pittsburgh, and that was half the reason I was scared and babbling—"

"Marissa." He squeezed her hand, his gaze so tender that she'd felt brave enough to pour out her heart even though she hadn't meant to. "I should have fought for you that night, but it hadn't sunk in that you were really planning to leave. I guess I thought right up until you walked away that I'd somehow make you change your mind."

"I try so hard to be practical when it comes to relationships and things between us just felt so out of control. So many feelings, so fast." But she didn't want to be practical anymore. She wanted to take a bold chance with a man worthy of the risk.

"I've got something for you that might help put your mind at ease." He dug into his pocket and slid a folded sheet of vellum across the table.

She recognized the crisp stationery from her office.

"A matchmaking questionnaire?" She remembered asking him to fill one out. One of her many deflections when he'd tried to get close to her.

"I thought it was time I wrote down everything I wanted in a relationship so you could see it on paper." He unfolded it for her and smoothed it out, then moved the candle closer so she could see the writing. "Maybe then you'll see how well we fit together."

He dragged his chair closer while she read aloud.

"Three most important qualities in a potential mate." Her finger followed the prompt to his neatly written answers. "Loyalty. A generous heart. Wears glasses."

She smiled, a warm glow filling her heart.

"Keep reading," he urged, pointing to the next question, his expression giving nothing away.

But by now, she guessed she was going to like what she saw.

"Are you emotionally available for a relationship, one (lowest) to ten (highest)." Again, she traced her way along the paper with a finger that now trembled. "You wrote in your own response, 'I am only available to Marissa Collins.'"

"See?" He took the paper from her and read a few other excerpts to her. "I'm also a sports enthusiast, but don't care if my potential mate goes to every game. I marked that I have a big family and only want to be with someone who understands the importance of family."

He paused and put the paper down. "That's you all over."

She nodded, speechless and overwhelmed, but in a very good way.

"Marissa, I want you by my side as my equal." He took her hand again and folded his fingers around hers, looking up at her in the glow of the candle and the stars. "If you can't go on the road with me, we'll find extra time to be together when I'm at home. If you want to come on the road, I'll make sure you fly home as often as you want. As often as you need to. I'm compensated too well for the job that I do and I'm happy to share that with someone who does a job as unselfish as yours."

"Kyle—" She gulped back a little yelp, so happy she still couldn't quite get the words out. She'd never expected such an outpouring from Kyle, the man who'd staunchly denied that he wanted a relationship when she'd tried to talk him into trying her matchmaking services. "That's so romantic."

"But it's practical, too," he insisted. "You weren't sure how it could work between us, but I'm willing to work hard and make plans to show you how it could happen so we're both happy and together as much as possible."

Marissa didn't have the eloquence that he did. So she laid her hand on top of his and took a deep breath.

"Yes." Once she got that much out, it freed the rest. "I want that, too."

The next thing she knew, she was in his arms, wrapped up tight, his strength and warmth all around her.

"You won't be sorry, Marissa. I promise." His whispered words in her ear sounded as happy and as relieved as she felt.

Nearby, a handful of players burst into wolf whistles and cheers. Axel Rankin whooped it up like a frat boy, jumping onto the stage with the band to take the microphone.

"Congratulations, Murph!" Turning the mic back over to the band, he left the stage and the pianist broke into the familiar strains of "At Last."

Marissa could hardly take it all in. Stacy jumped up and down beside Isaac's shoulder, shaking the camera he was trying to keep trained on Marissa and Kyle.

"Did they all know about this?" she asked, her face

buried in Kyle's white tuxedo shirt, his jacket long gone. He smelled so good, so familiar and so sexy. She couldn't wait to be with him. To begin a life together on their own terms.

"No. But I did tell Axel that I hoped to make up with you tonight. Possibly the rumor spread a little from there. It hasn't exactly been a secret how miserable I've been without you." He rose, bringing her to her feet along with him, his arms sliding around her waist.

"Your shots did look a little off without me around," she teased, liking the idea that she could take care of him and he'd take care of her back.

Just like it should be.

"It's tough to play when your heart is broken." He lifted one hand and kept the other around her waist, twirling her around while the lead singer belted out the romantic song.

"We're going to fix that," she assured him, her fingers skimming his chest.

"We're also going to have everything you want and more, including a guest house for your mom when she stops by to stay with us on her next cross-country tour."

"I'd like that." She prayed that would happen. The rehab staff had been really supportive of her idea for a new environment for her mom, helping Isaac find ways to tailor the three-dimensional images to the treatment center room.

"But I don't want you to sell your mom's house just for the sake of the medical bills. And if that means I have to buy it, I will." He twirled her again, giving her a moment to process the idea.

"Thank you," she said simply, accepting the gift for

her mother's sake as much as her own. She knew in her heart that this was going to work. She and Kyle wanted a future together too much to fail now. "Thank you so much."

Their song ended and a few of the partygoers whistled. Kyle and Marissa remained on the sidelines of the gathering, but Kyle lifted her hand in victory, claiming her in front of all his teammates. His coach. His brother.

"So I have tonight off," he said, turning to her again and pulling her flush up against him.

The warm rush of heat through her body was a heady feeling that—just a few days ago—she'd feared she might never feel again.

"Are you sure you don't need to go to bed early and rest up for a game?"

"Positive." He captured her chin in his hand and tilted her lips to his. "I want to spend the night with you."

"That can be arranged." She could almost taste him. "I know this great little spot where we can park the car and make out."

"What if I want to do more than kiss you?"

"I know a bed where you can have me any way you choose...."

And that's when the speed and strength of her superstar hockey player really paid off. He swept her off her feet, barreling through the crowd, to have her all to himself.

* * * * *

PASSION

Harlequin® Blaze

COMING NEXT MONTH
AVAILABLE APRIL 24, 2012

#681 NOT JUST FRIENDS
The Wrong Bed
Kate Hoffmann

#682 COMING UP FOR AIR
Uniformly Hot!
Karen Foley

#683 NORTHERN FIRES
Alaskan Heat
Jennifer LaBrecque

#684 HER MAN ADVANTAGE
Double Overtime
Joanne Rock

#685 SIZZLE IN THE CITY
Flirting with Justice
Wendy Etherington

#686 BRINGING HOME A BACHELOR
All the Groom's Men
Karen Kendall

REQUEST YOUR FREE BOOKS!
2 FREE NOVELS PLUS 2 FREE GIFTS!

Harlequin *Blaze*™

red-hot reads!

Julia McKee and Adam Sutherland never got along in college, but somehow, several years after graduation, they got stuck sharing the same bed on a weekend getaway with mutual friends. Can this very wrong bed suddenly make everything right between them?

Read on for a sneak peek from
NOT JUST FRIENDS by Kate Hoffmann.

Available May 2012, only from Harlequin® Blaze™.

"DO YOU REMEMBER the day we met?" Julia asked.

Adam groaned. "Oh, God, don't remind me. It was not my finest moment. My mind and my mouth were temporarily disengaged. I'd hoped you'd find me charming, but somehow, I don't think that was the case." He took her hand and pressed a kiss to her wrist, staring up at her with a teasing glint in his eyes.

Julia's gaze fixed on the spot where his lips warmed her skin. "Does that usually work on women?" she asked. "A little kiss on the wrist? And then the puppy-dog eyes?"

His smile faded. "You think I'm just playing you?"

"I've considered it," Julia said. But now that she saw the hurt expression on his face, she realized she'd been wrong.

She drew a deep breath and smiled. "I'm starving. Are you hungry?" Julia hopped out of bed, then grabbed his hand and pulled him up. "I can make us something to eat."

They wandered out to the kitchen, her hand still clasped in his, and when they reached the refrigerator, she pulled the door open and peered inside.

Grabbing a carton of eggs, she turned to face him. His hands were braced on either side of her body, holding the door open. Julia felt a shiver skitter over her skin.

Slowly, Adam bent toward her, touching his lips to hers. Julia had been kissed by her fair share of men, but it had never felt like this. Maybe it was the refrigerator sending cold air across her back. Or maybe it was just all the years that had passed between them and all the chances they'd avoided because of one silly slight on the day they'd met.

He drew back, then ran his hand over her cheek and smiled. "I've wanted to do that for eight years," he said.

Julia swallowed hard. "Eight?"

He nodded. "Since the moment I met you, Jules."

Find out what happens in NOT JUST FRIENDS
by Kate Hoffmann.

Available May 2012, only from Harlequin® Blaze™.

Harlequin *Presents*®

Royalty has never been so scandalous!

THE
SANTINA
CROWN

When Crown Prince Alessandro of Santina proposes
to paparazzi favorite Allegra Jackson it promises
to be *the* social event of the decade!

Harlequin Presents® invites you to step into the decadent
playground of the world's rich and famous and rub shoulders
with royalty, sheikhs and glamorous socialites.

**Collect all 8 passionate tales written by *USA TODAY*
bestselling authors, beginning May 2012!**

HP13066SC

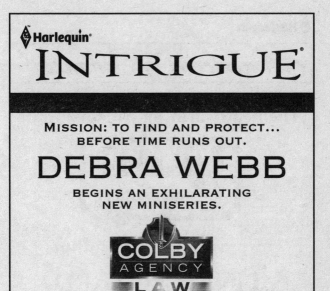